'A darkly mesmerising, fearless, and exquisitely written work. Stunning, harrowing, and brilliantly imagined.'
Emily St John Mandel, author of *Station Eleven*

'Each of these stories has its genesis in the question "What if...?" and Weinstein's imaginings are far too much like the current state of the world to be anything but chilling.' *Age*

'For lovers of the TV series *Black Mirror*, and anyone who racks up hours on Twitter, this is your short-story collection of the year.' *Electric Literature*

'[A] funny, discomfiting, and excellent debut…Even with a cursory reading of current events, it's difficult to deny that Weinstein's new world is the one our children will grow up in, if not the one we are already living in. Don't let anyone tell you these stories aren't real.' *Bomb Magazine*

'A bold debut…Weinstein deftly captures technology's limitations and leaves the reader to ponder the beauty found in the real world's imperfections. Ultimately, what is most remarkable, and chilling, about many of these stories is their resemblance to our current times.' *Bookpage*

'Disturbing, ludicrous and darkly humorous…Weinstein offers a thought-provoking take on a near-future about how advancement in technology will impact the way we live and connect as humans.' *Book Riot*

'In a world where technology is all-encompassing, *Children of the New World* seems to foreshadow the consequences…Each story takes on instances that may become very real in the future, making readers take a step back and question the effects of technology on our society.' *Signature*

'As we further allow ourselves to be infantilized by our amazing gadgets, Weinstein offers a counter-narrative that both warns us about a dangerous path and wallows in this freedom that unlocks immense pleasure and satisfaction.' *RollingStone.com*

'Storytellers like Alexander Weinstein come along once in a generation.' Stephen Parrish, editor of the *Lascaux Review*

'Taken together, these stories present a fully imagined vision of the future which will disturb you, provoke you, and make you feel alive. Weinstein is brilliant, incisive, and fearless.'
Charles Yu, author of *How to Live Safely in a Science Fiction Universe*

'In each of the gripping stories in *Children of the New World*, Alexander Weinstein offers a glimpse into an unnerving, not-so-distant and all-too-possible future. Weinstein explores the what-ifs with both wit and sensitivity, and his cautionary tales demand to be read (before it's too late).'
Judy Budnitz, author of *Nice Big American Baby*

'In Alexander Weinstein's debut collection, the future is a frightening and familiar place. Weinstein takes our uneasy truce with technology and blows it up, giving us child robots and ice worlds and the dark aftermath of failed revolutions. The collection is nothing short of a gorgeous new cold war, pitting us both with and against the science that threatens to become not-so-fictional every day.' Amber Sparks, author of *The Unfinished World: And Other Stories*

UNIVERSAL LOVE

Alexander Weinstein is the author of *Children of the New World*, which was named a notable book of the year by the *New York Times*, *NPR* and *Electric Literature*. He is a recipient of a Sustainable Arts Foundation Award, and his stories have appeared in *Best American Science Fiction and Fantasy* and *Best American Experimental Writing*. He is the director of the Martha's Vineyard Institute of Creative Writing and a professor of creative writing at Siena Heights University.

alexanderweinstein.com

UNIVERSAL LOVE

Stories

ALEXANDER WEINSTEIN

TEXT PUBLISHING MELBOURNE AUSTRALIA

The Text Publishing Company
Swann House, 22 William Street, Melbourne, Victoria 3000, Australia

The Text Publishing Company (UK) Ltd
130 Wood Street, London EC2V 6DL, United Kingdom

Some of these stories have appeared elsewhere, in slightly different form: 'True Love Testimonials' in *Southern Indiana Review* 26, no. 2 (Fall 2019); 'Mountain Song' in *Pleiades* 36, no. 2 (Summer 2016); and 'The Year of Nostalgia' in *Pleiades* 40, no. 1 (Winter 2020).

This is a work of fiction. All of the characters, organisations and events portrayed in this collection either are products of the author's imagination or are used fictitiously.

First published in the United States in 2020 by Henry Holt and Company
This edition published by The Text Publishing Company in 2020

Cover art and design by Tyler Comrie
Book design by Kelly S. Too

Printed and bound in Australia by Griffin Press, an accredited ISO/NZS 14001:2004 Environmental Management System printer

ISBN: 9781922268549 (paperback)
ISBN: 9781925923155 (ebook)

A catalogue record for this book is available from the National Library of Australia

This book is printed on paper certified against the Forest Stewardship Council® Standards. Griffin Press holds FSC chain-of-custody certification SGS-COC-005088. FSC promotes environmentally responsible, socially beneficial and economically viable management of the world's forests.

For my parents, Eva and Stephen

CONTENTS

UNIVERSAL LOVE

THE YEAR OF NOSTALGIA

I.

Nin found Dad frozen in the backyard. He wasn't trimming the hedges, just standing with his clippers in hand, staring at the bushes, she told me. Who knew how long he'd been like that, his body shivering. She'd put her hand on his back and guided him inside, where she made him a cup of tea.

"You need to come home, Leah," she said. So I asked for another week off, got a reluctant yes, and headed back to Ohio.

Our parents had done everything together, from puttering around the house to working in the garden. Dad would rake leaves, Mom would prepare lunch, and they'd sit in the living room in the late afternoon, reading ebooks together. At night they'd stream a movie or go into town for dinner. They were that rare and beautiful couple, almost nonexistent nowadays, lifelong companions and best friends. Then, suddenly, there was only Dad: calling to tell us Mom was gone, making funeral arrangements without us, stern-faced through the service, telling everyone he was fine, just fine.

I'd tried to help during the funeral—I cooked, cleaned the house, washed dishes, had planned to stay an extra week—but Dad pushed Nin and me away. Everything was fine, he told us, we girls should head home, no use staying at the house when we had our own lives to live. And after two days, he said we needed to go. What could we do? Nin left, driving the three hours back to her apartment in Toledo, and I flew back to Boulder, where Theo and the kids were waiting. Two weeks later, Nin called to tell me about finding Dad by the bushes.

Nin picked me up from the airport. Besides the funeral, the last time we'd been home together was when I was finishing my grad degree and she was completing her freshman year as an undergrad. We'd argued about something dumb—an anthropology course she hated—I'd called her narrow-minded, and she'd called me a patronizing bitch. After that we hadn't spoken for years. I was hoping grief might help us mend the distance, but when she picked me up she was being her annoying self, asking me about my flight while simultaneously flicking her eyes to send texts in her contacts as she drove.

"Uh-huh," she commented when I told her how the kids were doing, and laughed suddenly at a video in the corner of her eye. So, instead of continuing, I sat in the passenger seat hating how ADHD her generation was.

"If Dad's got dementia," she said, "you're going to have to move home. I can't handle this alone."

"He's just grieving," I said. I couldn't imagine uprooting everything and moving back to the Midwest. We had our jobs, the kids' school, never mind living in suburban Ohio, a place Nin might be able to survive but not a place I wanted to return to.

The house was a mess. Dad had let dishes pile up over the past weeks on tables, countertops, and bookshelves. Piles of laundry lay wherever he'd decided to get undressed. I ran the washing machine, scrubbed dishes, and mopped the floors while Dad told us he didn't need our help. Later that evening, we found him in the basement, standing by the water heater for some reason only he understood. I led him back upstairs and got him in bed while Nin mixed us drinks from a bottle of gin she'd found in the pantry. We sat at the kitchen table, exhausted. I scrolled through my eye-screens looking for advice about Dad while Nin played a dumb game on her retinas.

"What about Nostalgia?" I asked.

"That app came and went in the twenties," Nin said.

"Not according to this."

I blinked the article to her and she scanned it without stopping her game. "Whoa," she mumbled. "I had no clue old people were using it." She blinked me a hyperlink from the comment section, and soon my eyes were opening other related posts.

Like most people, I'd briefly subscribed to Nostalgia to get over a breakup. I'd uploaded videos of Sam, and there was his hologram making goofy jokes that made my heart leap. When I doubted my decision to dump him, I accessed the app's shadow side and suddenly his hologram was being his snarky old self, a dark cloud that confirmed how much better off I was without him. Nostalgia helped me get over Sam, but it also left me feeling clingy and pathetic, particularly on nights when I'd use a sex clip to get myself off to his ghost. Nin was more familiar with Nostalgia's reboot. She'd uploaded holograms of old friends to her contacts as a way to remember her high school days, before she grew bored and deleted the app.

But Nostalgia had changed since then, and we skimmed article after article, clicked on suggested posts, and finally went to bed long after midnight, appearing red-eyed the next morning at the breakfast table.

"Dad," we said, "we think we have a way to bring Mom back."

☀

We found Dad's contacts in a dusty case at the bottom of his dresser drawer. There were no daily videos on his feeds, no photos blinked from vacations, no live-memories of him and Mom gardening together. He'd only accessed his contacts for video calls, and had never explored the apps or used them for anything more complicated than a remedial form of Skype.

"Why would I want the world watching Mom gardening?" he asked.

"Maybe so we could have the memories," Nin said.

"You never took any photos?" I asked.

"Sure, plenty. On my phone."

"You're kidding, right?"

But it was true. Dad had used his old iPhone to snap pictures. We scrolled through the storehouse of megapixel selfies of him and Mom, the two of them posing like people did back at the start of the millennium. There were a few inexplicable portraits of them taken at such a far distance that there was no way it'd been a selfie stick.

"How'd you even get a shot like this?" Nin asked.

"We asked someone to take it."

I shrugged. "I guess people were more trusting back then."

Nostalgia was going to be a lot harder to use. There were drop-boxes to upload Dad's old pics to, user agreements, and clickable acknowledgments of less-than-perfect verisimilitude. It'd take twenty-four hours, which seemed forever, but it would be possible to re-create Mom from the photos.

To pass the time, Nin and I did the yard work that'd been neglected. We raked leaves in the autumn light, the trees an explosion of yellows and reds all around us. I tried to find a way to break the silence, but Nin was watching videos in her eyes and listening to music. She created small piles in the expanse of our backyard, then paused and stood there with her shoulders slumped. I went over and put my hand on her back.

"You okay?"

She closed her eyes. "Are you going to let her into your feed, too?"

I hadn't thought about it. "I guess I'll have to, right? Just to make sure it looks like Mom?"

"I think we both have to," she said. "That's going to be weird."

I pictured Mom again, her joy when we'd come home for the holidays. I didn't know how I'd respond to seeing her. Nin looked like she was about to cry, and I wanted to give her a hug, but she took her rake and walked across the yard to start on a corner we hadn't done yet, leaving us both to cope with our grief alone.

✳

Mom returned to us on a sunny Saturday afternoon. Dad, Nin, and I sat on the couch together, put in our contacts and logged on, and suddenly there she was, standing before us on the wooden floor.

"Leah," she said. "How are you, honey? Come give me a hug."

I looked to Nin. "I guess do it?" she said.

So I crossed the room and Mom leaned toward me, putting her holographic arms around me as though she were real. Then she called Nin up for a hug, and finally she sat down on the couch next to Dad. "Isn't it good to have the girls home, Lou!"

Our father didn't say anything, just looked at her, but his eyes were smiling.

"You know what we ought to do," she said, pulling a detail from some old photograph we'd uploaded. "We should carve a pumpkin tonight. What do you girls say?" She was up before we could answer, heading into the kitchen to do god knows what. We followed, and found her standing by the kitchen window, looking out at the yard. "Oh yes, we're definitely doing that tonight."

On her insistence we got the pumpkin, and all of us sat carving a jack-o'-lantern that evening. Mom knew a lot about Nin and me from the feeds we'd uploaded from our own contacts. She asked me about Theo and the kids, suggested we video-call them, but I lied and said they were watching a movie. I'd only started to explain Mom's death to them; this wasn't the time to let the boys speak with her hologram. If Mom worked, we'd prep the kids for a Christmas visit. But for now, with Mom suggesting we salt and roast pumpkin seeds, I wasn't sure what we were going to do. The hollowed gourd grinned at us from the table and we put a candle inside its bucktoothed mouth.

"Looks pretty spooky," Mom said.

Nin looked at me. "Sure does."

We stayed with Mom for another hour, but though she was clearly all intact, her hologram made me feel as though something was missing, an arm or a leg. Nin looked like she was going to be sick. So we said we were tired, and I gave Mom an air hug good night before putting

my arms around Dad. "You sure you're okay with this?" I
asked as we hugged.

"Thank you," he said into my ear. Then he thanked
Nin, his contacts looking damp in the kitchen light, and
we left him and Mom sitting at the kitchen table chatting.
Later, we heard them turn on the TV to stream a movie
together, and Nin and I went to bed, wondering if we'd
made the right decision.

⁘

At four in the morning, we heard the garbage cans being
dragged down the driveway. I opened my curtains to see
Dad outside in the frosted night, wrestling with the leaves
we'd bagged by the curb. He lifted one of the large paper
bags, spilling leaves everywhere as he tried to stuff it into
the yard waste container. A couple doors down the neighbor's dog began barking.

By the time we got outside Dad was in the garage,
yanking a rake off the wall. Nin and I stood in the bleak
garage light. "Dad, what are you doing?" I asked.

His hand gripped the rake as if he might take a swing
at us. "You can't just leave the bags like that."

"Dad," Nin said. "You're freezing. Come inside—"

"It'll rain, they'll rip."

"Dad," Nin tried again.

"You girls don't know how to take care of anything."
He tried to circle around us, but Nin put her hand on his
arm to keep him from leaving.

"Dad," she said. "Where's Mom?"

I blinked on my contacts and logged into Nostalgia. As far as I could see, Mom was still upstairs in their bed. Dad let out a white breath in the winter darkness, his knuckles blue around the rake.

"You girls made a mess," he huffed.

"We're sorry," I said, and Nin took his arm softly.

"Come on, Dad. We'll make you some coffee, okay? You can tell us how to take care of the leaves."

Dad didn't move, but his grip on the rake loosened. Then he looked past us toward the curb and all the leaves scattered there. "You made a goddamned mess."

Inside, Nin and I sat bleary-eyed as Dad held his mug between his hands and told us that the woman upstairs wasn't his wife.

"We know," Nin said. "That's what we were trying to tell you. It's just a hologra—"

"She's a damned kindergarten teacher."

"Huh?" I asked.

"You're all up early," Mom said, walking into the kitchen. "What's the celebration, sleepyheads?"

"She's not my wife," Dad repeated, oblivious to Mom without his contacts.

Mom began humming a song from our childhood. "What would you girls like for breakfast? Some chocolate-chip pancakes?"

"I think we better log her out," Nin whispered. So we did and Mom was gone, her humming cut mid-note. Dad's hands were shaking. I reached out and put my palms on his fists. "Explain it to us again," I said.

It took a while, Dad mostly repeating that Mom wasn't his wife—which didn't make sense to either of us—but finally it began to grow clear: the nursery rhymes, the chocolate-chip pancakes, the singsong voice she'd slip into. The only recorded video feeds we'd uploaded had been Nin's and my own, most of them from when we were kids. Mom's hologram was closer to our childhood mother than the wife Dad knew, and though she'd entertained him last night with her novelty, after we went to bed she'd only wanted to talk about building a snowman together this winter.

We logged on to Nostalgia for an emergency hotline or email help center but found nothing. There was no contact form or FAQ page—just a stupid little cartoon fox that kept popping up in the corner of my vision and asking, *What can I fox out for you?*

"How do you get rid of that fucking fox?"

"I think the fox is our only hope," Nin said. So I right-blinked on him and thought-typed a short question. The reply came seconds later.

I'm sorry you're having trouble with your mother. Can you describe the problem? —Devi

We told Devi our mom was stuck in a childhood loop.

Can your dad please upload his feeds? This should fix the problem.

Our father has no feeds, we thought-typed.

OK! Do you have access to other social media? Blog posts your mother has written, personal websites, maybe an old Instagram account?

No, we told him, our mom didn't even have a smart-phone. Wasn't there anything else we could use?

Archive Services is a good match! Our compassion-based AIs will reconstruct your mother from textual materials. Click here for a link on how to scan and upload diaries and journals.

Diaries? Journals? Those were things people wrote in ancient times. But when we asked Dad, he said there might be something in a trunk in the basement. Sure enough, below the stairs, inside a musty wooden chest, was an archive of our mother's life. There were finger paintings we'd made when we were five, first-grade report cards, and the yellowed edges of printed-out emails our parents had sent each other. The lion's share, however, were forty-odd bound journals.

"What are these?" I asked, picking one from the top.

"Your mom wrote in those before bed."

"Can we have them?" Nin asked.

"Sure," Dad said before turning to go back upstairs, leaving us with our mother's secret life. Nin opened one of the journals. *Nin called from college asking for money. Always the same: more money, more plane tickets, more donations for some stupid sorority thing.*

"Jeez," Nin said. "Nice, Mom."

"Yeah, well, read this." I showed her lines from the journal I'd opened. *He wanted me to touch him, but I wasn't in the mood. Still, decided to do something. Told him to lie perfectly still and . . .*

"Ugh," Nin said. She handed me back the journal. "Wait, that's Dad she's writing about, right?"

I scanned the pages and grimaced. "Yeah," I said, and shut the book.

"Well, there's plenty here," Nin said, "but you've got to be kidding me. We need to scan all these? It'll take forever."

Which was what Devi told us when we clicked back on the fox. Yes, we could do it, blinking photos of every page and uploading the files one by one, but that would be a complete nightmare. For an additional fee, Nostalgia's scanner-bots would do everything for us. If we blinked the Order Now button, an overnight mailer would arrive within the hour. Simply put the materials in the box, return it to the driver, and they'd take it from there. It only required a one-year commitment plus a per-page scanning fee. Everything, he assured us, was insured against loss. It was expensive, but Dad needed help, and I needed to get home. So we blinked the ArchivePlus Membership, and sure enough the FedEx boxes arrived within the hour.

"I'll pack everything," Nin said.

"It's okay, I'll do it," I told her. Sending Mom's valuable treasures across the country seemed risky and Nin was only ever half-there. She was rolling her eyes to delete text messages while watching some stupid video in her peripheral vision. Would she even attach the mailing labels correctly?

"Leah, I'm not dumb. I got this. Go take care of Dad."

I took a deep breath. Nin and I were starting to get along after all these years of silence. *Don't be a patronizing bitch,* I told myself. So I left her in the basement with the boxes and went upstairs to see if Dad was hungry.

Nostalgia received our boxes that evening. Devi sent us hourly updates that showed the percentage of journals the scanner-bots had uploaded, and he guided us through the setup once everything was complete.

Loved ones often have memories better left unknown, Devi warned us. *Affairs, addictions, abuse. It sounds like your father's in a vulnerable state?*

"Yes," we told him.

I suggest using Parental Controls. Our AIs have created folders from your mother's history so you can tailor your mom to your family's preference. For an extra charge, you can add up to three users, each with customizable profiles. You'll each have the mother you'd like to remember!

We scrolled through the categories. *Legal. Romance. Drugs & Alcohol.* I considered the brief glimpse we'd had of our parents' sex life. Sure, we let him know—we each wanted our own accounts. Nin clicked on Legal. There were some parking tickets and a DUI that neither of us knew about. I clicked on Romance. Next to the checked box for our father was a long list of names. *Rodrigo, Shane, Desert Dog, Antonio . . .*

"What the fuck?"

Devi was telling us about how to stylize our individual profiles to better match our memories, but we were already scrolling through the names.

"*Who are these guys?*" Nin asked.

"Do you think Dad knew about this?"

"I don't know . . . but, I mean . . . jeez . . ."

Do you want to use Parental Controls on your father's account? Devi asked.

"Yes!" we both said. So Devi set up a password that only Nin and I could unlock.

Okay, just customize your father's access to be closest to his memories, and you'll be ready to launch!

We thanked Devi and looked again at all the men's names, then the Drugs & Alcohol folder with its many boxes for whisky, wine, cigarettes, and weed. "I guess we have to somehow ask Dad about all this," I said.

Dad was downstairs at the kitchen table where he spent most of his days, drinking coffee and playing games on his phone. "Dad?" we asked. "We're trying to fix Mom, but we have to ask you a couple questions. Did Mom have a lot of boyfriends before you two met?"

"She had a high school sweetheart and a guy she dated in college, why?"

We clicked on *Romance*, unchecked all the guys, and gave our father access only to the box for himself.

"What about drugs? Did you guys party a lot when you were younger?"

"We had a glass of wine from time to time."

"What about cigarettes, marijuana, Ecstasy, cocaine?"

"*What kinds of questions are these?* No. She liked wine coolers."

We opened the Drugs & Alcohol file and disabled his access.

We made it through a couple more difficult questions, and finally gave him limited access: only to the person he'd known our mother to be. Then Nin extended his contact case to him.

"I'm not putting those back in."

"Dad," she said. "Just try it one more time. We promise, if it's not like Mom you'll never have to use these again."

Dad sat there, looking at the lenses. Then, finally, one by one, he placed them on his eyes and we logged on with him.

"Hon," Mom said. She was standing in the doorway between the kitchen and living room. "What are you moping around the kitchen table for? Come on, let's take our walk."

"How's she know about our walks?" Dad asked.

"Lou, you better not be going senile, it's what we do every day. Come on, get your coat."

Dad looked at us, then back at Mom. "I guess we're going for a walk."

They were gone for over an hour, and when they got back Dad still had his contacts in, his fingers embedded within her holographic skin as if holding her hand. That afternoon, they worked together in the yard. I looked out the kitchen window and saw Dad standing by the back hedge with his clippers, talking to Mom. I blinked off

Nostalgia and suddenly there he was, standing by himself, talking to the empty space by his side like a crazy person. We'd have to tell the neighbors about Mom's hologram, but for the first time since the funeral I felt like maybe things weren't going to keep sliding toward some awful place.

That night at dinner, Mom talked up a storm, being her usual self. After we were done, Dad said that maybe it was time for him and Mom to go to bed. They walked upstairs, and as Nin and I cleaned up the kitchen and turned on the dishwasher, we heard them talking in their bedroom.

"Seems like it's working," I said.

"Guess we'll know at four in the morning."

I sighed. "She really seemed like Mom."

"Ya," Nin said. "Seeing her is super weird. I can't even feel sad anymore."

"I know. It's like she never died. I guess that's the point, right?"

"I guess," Nin said.

"You want a hug?" And when she didn't answer, I put my arms around her.

"Just promise you'll come back if this doesn't work," Nin said.

"Of course," I said, still holding her. And we stood there in the light of the kitchen while upstairs our parents talked, our whole family together beneath the same roof again.

II.

Life began to move quickly after I returned to Boulder. I went back to my job, worked on clients' websites, and called Dad daily, but he was always anxious to get off the phone. "One sec, your mom's calling me," he'd say. Then, "Gotta go—call you back later," and I wouldn't hear from him until I called again.

Whenever I did get to speak to him for more than a couple minutes, he sounded happy. He was busy with things around the house; he'd joined a Nostalgia bowling league and every week he and a group of other widowed men bowled together with their dead wives. Mom was busy getting all her online Christmas cards in order, and Dad was about to get started on redoing the roof of the garage.

"Mom's really good?" I asked.

"Yeah, yeah," he said. "I can't thank you girls enough. It's good to have her company. And there's a lot I never knew about her!"

"Oh?" I said, worried. "Like what?"

"She's funny. Not that she wasn't before—but it's like . . . well . . . she's just being more of herself around me."

"Wasn't she always herself?"

"Not like this. She's different but in a good way," he said. "And what spunk! That's her now." He had to get off the phone, they were about to go ice skating.

All this I took as a good sign. Nin texted to say she'd

visited and Dad was doing fine. There were no more epi-
sodes of finding him frozen with grief, and soon things
felt like how they'd been before Mom's death, all of us
busy with our lives. We had our first snowstorm, the
kids got the flu, and Nin called to say she'd gotten the
journals back from Nostalgia—everything was safe in
the trunk.

"Did you read them?" I asked.

"Um, I'm cool without knowing about Mom and
Dad's sex life."

"What about those other guys in her folders—did you
open those?"

"Seriously, Leah, do you really want to know if Mom
was having an affair with a guy named Desert Dog?"

"No," I said, though the list gnawed at me. Nin and
I had explored her Alcohol & Drugs folder. Apparently,
in her youth Mom had smoked a lot of hash in Europe,
drunk tequila with a ranchero in Mexico, and regularly
smoked cigarettes. Nin and I quizzed Dad about it. Was
he sure Mom had never smoked? Never, he told us. Never
drunk bourbon? He laughed. All Mom ever had was an
occasional glass of white wine, he insisted.

We both wanted the Mom we remembered, so Nin
and I agreed to leave those folders unopened. Still, I
couldn't believe Nin wouldn't at least skim the journals,
but I stopped myself from saying anything. I let her tell
me about her dating life instead, and I told her about
Theo and the kids, and though I wanted to ask her to send
me all of Mom's journals, I didn't. There was no point in

taking a second chance of losing them in the mail, I'd pick them up when we visited Dad for Christmas.

"Have you been accessing Mom?" I asked.

"No," Nin said. "I keep her logged out when I visit Dad. It's weird to watch him just talking to himself, but I'm not comfortable seeing her hologram."

I knew what she meant. Being with Mom, even for those couple of days, had sealed my grief somewhere deep inside. I could feel the tears wanting to come, but my throat wouldn't let them out. One day Mom had been alive, the next she was gone, and then she was back as a hologram, her whole life sorted for us in online folders.

That night, after Theo was snoring, I lay awake wondering what Dad had meant. *Mom was funny? Better than before?* And what about the fact that there was a folder specifically labeled *Italian Men?* It was two in the morning when I got out of bed, pulled on sweatpants and my jacket, and slid open the patio door.

The Flatirons rose high behind our house, capped with snow that glowed silver in the moonlight, the stars shimmering above them. I rolled my eyes to the right and blinked open Nostalgia. Then I went to my user profile of Mom, accessed the folders, and checkmarked them all. *Are you sure you want to enable Full Access?* My breath emerged in small white clouds. Yes, I wanted to know who my mother really was. So I blinked and brought Mom back to life for the first time since I'd come home.

"Hey, hon," she said. In the evening light her hologram looked as real as flesh. "It's late. What's wrong?"

"I was just thinking about you."

"I know you better than that. What's the matter?"

"Well . . ." I said, trying to find the right words. "I just want to know some things about you. Stories from your life you never told me, like who you were before you had us."

"Ha!" she laughed. "That's the first time you've ever wanted to hear about that." Her hologram passed through the back of the deck chair and sat down in it. She crossed one leg over the other, looking more relaxed than I'd ever seen her, and dug around in her jacket. Then she brought out a pack of cigarettes and a lighter, shook a cigarette free and lit it.

"Mom, you smoke?"

"Mm-hm," she said, looking out at the mountains as she took a long drag. "So," she asked through the white exhalation of her holographic smoke, "what do you want to know?"

The winter of Mom, as I came to call it, was the year Nostalgia made a comeback. Nin, Dad, and I were merely the crest of a larger wave. Retirement homes held Reunion Socials where seniors danced with long-lost loved ones, and the news ran human-interest stories, showing clips of widowers twerking by themselves in ballrooms. Around town, men sat on park benches having conversations with lost buddies. And at Whole Foods, a woman was cooing to her shopping cart. When I reached past

her for a jar of tomato sauce, she looked at me sheep-
ishly. "My son's a teenager now," she explained. "I miss
his toddler years."

Nostalgia had finally become what it'd always been
meant for—a way to help us cope—and Mom's return to my
life didn't seem strange or pathetic, like my holographic
sex sessions of yesteryear, but rather a way to reconnect
with her. In the evenings, before Theo got home, Mom
and I would sit together on the back porch, and she shared
an inner life with me that she'd never shown to anyone
in our family.

"Did you know I went to Italy?" she asked. "It was a
wild decision—my dorm mate and I found cheap tickets and a small hotel in Sicily. Your grandparents hated
the idea, but I went anyway. There was a vineyard—the
family had owned it for hundreds of years—we ate cured
olives and drank Chianti, and there was a cute boy who
worked in the winery. I drank a whole bottle of wine with
him in the fields one night. We were free, and tipsy, and
full of life. He said he loved me, and in those rows of
grapevines we kissed all through the summer nights. He
had these gorgeous brown curls and deep dark eyes. The
night before I left Italy, I snuck into his room at the villa
and we held each other until the blue light of morning
leaked in his window. Oh, Leah, I shouldn't be telling you
this; you must be mortified."

"Mom, it's okay. Really, I'm not embarrassed." Which
was true. Even though it was my mother sitting there,
I knew I was glimpsing someone else. Someone full of

passion and hope. A woman who had nothing to do with me, or Nin, or Dad.

"Can I tell you a secret?" Mom asked, and I nodded. "I've been with your father for almost forty years, but I still think about that boy. As we lay in bed that last morning, he invited me to see a movie. And I told him I'd love to, but our plane was leaving in the afternoon. *Then stay with me*, he said. And, Leah, of course I wouldn't give up the life I chose, I'm happy how things turned out, I love your father, but sometimes I can't help but wonder what it would've been like if I'd just stayed there at the height of summer when life and love were fully blooming."

"You're more poetic than I ever knew," I said.

"Ha! How much money do you need to borrow?" She took a drag of her cigarette. "Well, truth is, I always wanted to be a poet."

"Really?"

"I thought I'd write a great book. Might still."

"Yeah, Mom, you should do that."

The sun was setting and the Flatirons were framed in golden light. "It's beautiful here," Mom said. "You did good moving to Colorado, your job, Theo and the kids. But tell me, are you happy?"

"Yeah," I said quickly.

"Honey," Mom said. She leaned forward, letting her cigarette dangle over her knee. "I mean *really* happy. Are you making memories with Theo?"

"I think so," I said, though truthfully I wasn't sure. I loved the kids, loved Theo. We had good jobs, a nice home, we were happy. But there were also these long stretches of sameness. We planned trips and they'd finally arrive, but even our vacations were filled with to-do lists, packing and unpacking, the kids throwing tantrums— and we'd return home to bedtime schedules, lunches to pack, and dishes, dishes, dishes. Throughout all that, there were moments of grace. Like how sometimes, in bed after the kids were asleep, Theo and I would look at each other in the darkness as though we were new to one another. And, sure, there were moments of passion, but they seemed too few. I told Mom all this as well as I could, sharing things with her that until that moment I'd never expressed even to myself.

"Listen to me, Leah," Mom said. "You have to live with adventure. Life is too precious to waste."

"I'm trying," I said, and suddenly I felt my grief give way and a sob broke from my throat, followed by another.

"Oh, Leah," Mom said, holding out her arms. "Come here." And though I couldn't hold on to anything besides the back of her deck chair, I reached out, held on, and she put her arms around me. "You let everything out."

So, I did. I grieved for her and for myself; I wept and wept until I'd made myself a snotty, teary mess on our patio in the winter dusk. I wiped my eyes on my sleeve.

"Mom?"

"Yes, honey," she said, her hologram looking at me in the evening light.

"I'm so happy you're back."

That winter, I became aware of life again. Mom, in her death, was helping me understand that everyone carried around an inner world they never shared. Me, Theo, Nin, Dad—we all kept secret lives. But with Mom there was no hiding and no fear. Her death had liberated a kind of truth between us, and within that openness Mom told me more about herself. How, long before my father, she'd ridden horses in Mexican canyons and sat beneath desert stars listening to the sound of blazing saguaro and coyotes baying with chilling howls. She'd met a man there, a young ranchero, who'd saved her from a flash flood in the middle of a thunderstorm as the water ripped through the Sierra Madres. All of it sounded wild and beautiful. There was a passionate earthiness to my mother that was so distant from the Midwestern housewife I'd known.

We were driving back from getting groceries, making our way up Arapahoe toward the mountains. Mom was sitting in the empty seat beside me, watching thick snowflakes fall against our windshield, layering the streets white. It felt like the first flurries of a big storm, the kind that quietly piles up overnight and transforms Boulder into a city of igloos by morning. I watched her out of the corner of my eye, realizing I'd never really known who she was when she was alive. Mom's life was filled with romance and passion—things clearly integral to who she was. Why, of all the people in this world, did it seem like I knew nothing about her? Hadn't she ever planned to share those stories with us? I asked her.

"You were busy with your own lives," she said. "You didn't have time for stories about my romantic adventures! Then you were in college, and grad school, then building a life with Theo and the kids."

"But why didn't you just tell me anyway?" I asked.

"Honey," she said and lit a cigarette in the car. "You never seemed that interested in my life."

And, for the first time, I understood that I hadn't been.

III.

We went home to see Dad that Christmas. We explained Mom's hologram to the kids, told them how, just like the holographic games they played and the invisible Lego castles they constructed, Mom wasn't actually real. Then we paid the extra money to add another two profiles to our account, hid all the sex, drugs, and alcohol, and let the boys log on with Grandma for a couple hours each day to prepare them for the upcoming visit.

The kids loved her. Even Theo had to admit that Nostalgia wasn't as bad as he'd first thought. The boys could have their grandmother back, and we could have some alone time while she played with them in the living room. On the plane to Ohio, we were lucky to find a row with an

empty seat, and we logged Mom on so she could enter-
tain the boys while we napped.

Nin picked us up from the airport, and we talked on
the ride back. Ever since Mom had returned, I felt closer
to Nin. For the first time in over a decade it seemed as
though we were actually sisters again. She had a new boyfriend, she told me. He was home in Connecticut for the
holidays, so at night she'd excuse herself and sneak off to
holo-chat with him.

The house looked good. Mom couldn't clean, but
she'd taught Dad to. Gone were the dirty dishes and piles
of clothing we'd found during his weeks of grieving,
and Dad had paid the extra money for Christmas Décor
uploads so Mom could decorate. Though the living room
looked no different with our contacts out, when we
logged on, there was the Christmas tree glowing bright
with white lights, ornaments, and intricately cut snowflakes in all the windows.

"She bosses me around, but we have fun!" Dad said as
he put the turkey in the oven.

On Christmas morning we sang carols together and
opened presents. Mom and Dad had bought the kids a
hologame called Crossbows & Catapults, which Theo fell
in love with. He and the boys built huge fortresses in the
living room and launched flaming cannonballs at one
another that the rest of us couldn't see. Dad was entertained by Mom, Nin had her boyfriend's hologram to talk
to, the children had their games, and I caught up on some
videobooks that I'd wanted to watch for months. It was,

in many ways, the first truly stress-free holiday we'd had in years.

Being back with Dad's version of Mom made me realize how different she was around him. At first I mistook the difference as a kind of tightness, as though she was uncomfortable—but then I realized it was her posture. With Dad, she sat with both legs straight, her knees forward, reserved and less relaxed, but in Boulder, she'd crossed one leg over the other as she smoked, looking almost like she was posing for an old film poster. Dad's limited version of Mom was odd, and I missed the Mom I knew—the one who'd gotten drunk in Rome and danced her way up the Spanish Steps. At night, when everyone was busy with their contacts, I'd go for walks along the frosted streets with my own version of Mom. We'd walk the subdivision as Mom smoked her evening cigarette, and I'd listen to more of her stories. Then I'd log her out before coming back inside to the other Mom who was sitting in the living room, watching TV, suggesting we make cookies.

We stayed on for New Year's, cooked lobsters, and after dinner everyone hung out in the living room, entertained by their private holograms as we waited for the ball to drop. Theo played the Crossbows game with the kids; Nin was in her old bedroom, talking to her new boyfriend's projection; and Dad sat next to Mom on the couch. They laughed and held hands in their limited way.

"I think I'll go downstairs to look at Mom's journals," I told Theo.

"Sounds good," he said, half-listening. He let an invisible cannonball fly and the kids cheered.

When I opened the trunk, Nin's mess greeted me like a slap. Mom's journals were scattered everywhere, clearly dumped in, the printed-out emails crumpled by their weight. I sighed. Nin and I might be growing closer, but she was still as immature as ever. I picked up a couple of the letters, flattened them with my hand, and stacked them by the side of the trunk. Then I picked up one of the journals and opened it.

Horrible mood. Kids plain awful. Nin threw a tantrum, wanted some cereal she'd seen on TV. Leah acting lofty and condescending at the supermarket. "No, put it back," she said. As though she's the mother. I ended up yelling at them.

I flipped to another section about a movie she and Dad had watched. *Pretty good. Not my favorite but Lou liked it. Think he just liked the young girl detective.* There was no poetry or hot teenage romance as far as I could see—just pages upon pages of a discussion she and Dad were having about remodeling the kitchen. I put the journal on the floor, picked up another one, and began reading about a new type of potpourri Mom liked. I put the journal down and picked up another, then another. There were no Italian lovers, no runaway horses, no midnight kisses. The most sexy it got was a single line: *Lou and I had sex tonight.* Otherwise it was just Mom, sounding like Mom: a nice woman who was overworked by the daily tasks of raising us and exhausted by it all.

I dug through the chest for an older-looking journal

and saw, buried near the bottom, a picture of a woman in a see-through negligée next to a table with two empty wineglasses. I put the journal down and reached for the book. *Chianti Dreams*, the title of the paperback read. Behind the wineglasses, the setting sun illuminated a perfect silhouette of a curly-haired Italian man with his shirt open. I turned the book over. *It was supposed to be a summer college trip, but after she meets Antonio, Suzette's life will never be the same. Ravenous for love and adventure, Suzette finds the kind of love that will soon be forbidden.*

"What the fuck?" I said aloud. I skimmed the pages, and found Suzette, a woman who lay in beds with Italian men in the turquoise light of morning, and crossed her legs seductively while smoking cigarettes. I dug through the chest and found another thick gaudy paperback, the kind one might find in the magazine aisle of Meijer's. *South of the Border*. A shirtless ranchero stood illuminated by lightning, his pecs streaked with rain as he held on to a dark-haired woman.

The door opened from above.

"Babe, you coming up? It's almost midnight."

I heard the kids squealing upstairs and Nin in the kitchen asking where the champagne was. I laid the paperback down atop the journal and shut my eyes, imagining the scanner-bots in some distant warehouse committing every item of Nin's rushed packing to holographic memory.

Upstairs, Nin had placed a bunch of wineglasses and the unopened champagne bottle by the edge of the coffee table while she talked to her holographic boyfriend. "I'll totally toast with you! We're about to open the champagne!" she told no one in the room.

"Hey, babe," Theo said, and gave me a kiss. "My sister's streaming from Oakland." He gestured to the empty space at his side. "Want to blink her in and say hi?"

But I didn't want to see any more holograms. "Just say hello from me," I told him.

Our kids were in the corner playing their hologame, their eyes transfixed by whatever they were setting fire to, and my father was turned toward my mother, his eyes wet with joy. But Mom was gone. I'd logged her off on my way up from the basement. It was just my father turning toward the empty space, preparing to kiss the air. In the corner of our eyes, a projection of a young Dick Clark was starting the countdown from Times Square. Millions of partiers were beaming from across the nation, singing the first bars of "Auld Lang Syne" as the ball descended in New York. Theo laughed at something his sister said, Nin popped the champagne and kissed the empty air, and we stood there, in the last seconds of the old year, counting down the time together.

BEIJING

The sandstorms had returned from Mongolia, bringing with them a suspension of dust so thick it layered silt against the sides of buildings and swallowed high-rises within yellow clouds. The dust settled amid the strati of plastic fumes which stretched across the apartment, coating Gabriel's throat with sand and reminding him of that winter, before he'd left for China, when his brother had pushed his face into a snowbank and nearly killed him. He opened his mouth in bed, gasping for oxygen, and had a dreamlike vision of melting animals, their fur singed, their backs arching in blue flame—was certain he would die here alone in Beijing—but then he caught a breath, thin as fishing line, and sipped at the rivulet of clean air. Yes, if he practiced the *pranayama* he and David had once done together, he could rise from bed and dress.

He tried the switch on the wall again, waited to hear the air tanks whir to life, but there was nothing. Only angry voicemails left at a realty company in Hong Kong, and the company's reminder that he lived in a good building—an apartment with working oxygen over half the year, a unit that the company could easily evict him from. But, if he breathed slowly and deeply, as he was doing, maybe he could make it from his apartment to the train station. There'd be clean air on the train to Shanghai, and this thought buoyed Gabriel's spirits.

He'd heard from his brother for the first time in three years. Jake would be visiting Shanghai on business and had asked Gabriel to meet him at his hotel; they needed to talk about their parents, he'd said. Shanghai was a six-hour journey from Beijing, but Jake had hinted that he might be willing to buy Gabriel a ticket back to the United States, and this possibility of escape was enough to help Gabriel make it down the staircase to the front door.

The air outside made Gabriel's eyes water and his lungs ache. The electric plant had browned out and a stench of dead fish filled the city. Regulars passed with face masks and personal air tanks, off to work in the skyscrapers that disappeared within the yellow haze. Next to a public toilet was a working air station. The stations sat like lily pads throughout the city, a dozen face masks attached to municipal-grade air. When the tanks were new and properly maintained, the commute to work was manageable. But too often the city forgot to refill them, or teenagers found it funny to piss into the masks, and he'd put the face cradle on only to inhale the ammoniac stench. Today, however, none of the face masks smelled of urine and all the tanks except one had been refilled. Gabriel made it from lily pad to lily pad, waiting only once by the tanks closest to the train station, where an old man sat breathing slowly through a working mask, the back of his suit rising and falling like a wounded moth. Then the old man rose and went zigzagging into the crowd, fluttering like a drunk through early-morning commuters, and Gabriel placed the mask over his mouth and took his last breaths of Beijing air.

David had called the technicians sacred healers—said the way they tracked the branching tunnels of neurons was a kind of magic. They found trenches deep within the brain worn thin by traumatic memories and filled them with the electronic spackle of pure light.

"Wherever there's an open passageway of depression, they patch it," David promised.

They were at another after-work soiree, the party at Sheraton's VIP lounge, thrown by a visiting holographer to promote his latest watch. There were dragon-fruit cocktails and neon hookahs smoking from dimly lit tables, while high above the crowd, neuro-technicians stood like go-go dancers beside illuminated lounge chairs where they gave partyers microsurgeries, repairing the wrinkled brows of executives' bad memories as quickly as giving a shot of Botox. Gabriel was buzzed on lychee mojitos, watching the young techies patch up the partygoers' pain. The music changed to AcidHop and a woman came down the spiral staircase, radiant from forgetting.

"Come on, let's get patched!" David yelled over the music.

"I told you, I don't want to."

"Suit yourself."

David let go of Gabriel and climbed the circular staircase to the waiting technicians. Beneath the pounding beats of the DJ, the neurosurgeon leaned over David with his light drill, bored open the pathways to his pain, and filled them with electronic spackle, and Gabriel wondered if he should've gone, too. Earlier, he'd remained limp when David took him in his mouth. Maybe the surgeon could patch that memory? And what about the other memories? Like his anger over David's constant patching, or the terror of their dwindling savings, or how almost every night David was going to another event, spending more money, claiming *networking* was good for them. Just last week, to cut back on costs, they'd stopped buying air tanks. Could the surgeons patch those memories? And if they did, would his body respond as it once had when David held him?

"Good to go!" the nanotech yelled, bouncing to the beat of the music, and David rose from his chair and sauntered down the staircase. When he saw Gabriel, he threw his arms around his neck. Gone were David's memories of the fight they'd had before the party, gone the cold tone from his voice; there was just his body pressed against Gabriel's as they danced and danced and danced.

Back outside, the party was a glowing pulse far above, everything submerged in fog as they walked. The lights of apartment windows looked like portholes on passing submarines. A single red light bled through the exhaust of Beijing's endless traffic, and in his post-patched joy, David said it was the eye of some great beast watching over them as they made their way home. The traffic reminded Gabriel of a sliding-gem puzzle with its single missing square, the drivers waiting for a piece to move so they might finally advance. Inside one of the cars was a young man—his hands falling from the wheel, his wife sleeping beside him, their two children looking pale as they suffocated within the fish tank of the automobile. The light changed and an enormous bus began a wide turn, making it a couple feet before blocking the intersection and sending a refrain of honks into the night. David danced past the bus, and where two cars were bumper-to-bumper he put his hands against the trunk of one and the hood of the other and jumped over them. Gabriel climbed over clumsily, waving in apology to the driver who was honking at him, at David, at the bus, at the world.

At home, David pressed him against the wall of their apartment. "I fucking love you," he said, and kissed him. Being drunk helped Gabriel's pain. The fight they'd had was a murky recollection. Instead there was just the post-patched evening spread out like a beautiful film—David

dancing, David laughing, David kissing him in public—
and Gabriel promised himself that the next time they
arrived to the club fresh from a fight, he'd consider climbing into the technician's chair and letting the neurosur-
geons make him as happy as David was.

Fumes choked the railway platform, and Gabriel worried
he'd pass out like he'd done last week when running late
to work. He'd forgone two air stations before the sky had
filled with tiny fireflies and he'd found himself on his
back, a passerby's mask over his mouth.

He mashed alongside the businessmen shoving their
way toward the open doors of the train and wedged
his elbow in front of an old woman who was using an
enormous bag to cut in line. The doors closed behind
him, new air blew into the cabin, and Gabriel raised his
face to the vents and tasted the compressed air, taking
long, deep breaths as he closed his eyes. By the time he
opened them again, Beijing was gone. Now only the red-
tiled houses and battered fields of Tianjin remained. A
rusted crane stretched over an unfinished soccer stadium,
useless and dead, and around it, tall buildings rose win-
dowless and half-finished. Metal skeletons of electrical
towers stood spread-legged across the landscape, their
fists clutching cables as they held guard over New China.

The holograph businesses had arrived here like a plague
of locusts, devouring the land, poisoning the drinking
water, and leaving behind suburbs with hungry people

playing on the outdated gadgets they'd once built for Americans. Here you could get thought-phones aplenty for pennies on the dollar. And there were no cherry trees left, just the horrible super-trees, strung with toilet paper and windswept plastic bags, which blossomed holographic flowers when they were still functioning but now stood broken along the streets. The entire landscape was a mausoleum of failed construction projects. As for the vultures of industry, they'd moved elsewhere—to Nigeria, some said, just as they'd once said Tianjin, just as they'd said Beijing before that.

When they'd moved to China, David had promised they'd take a trip to Shanghai to hear the monks singing sacred mantras before the golden statues of Buddha. They'd sit by the Bodhi tree, hold each other's hands, and meditate as they'd done back in Bloomington's Zen center, where they'd met, both hoping to fill the darkness of their histories with light. David had said he knew a company that promised quick riches programming holographic apps. The website advertised a beautiful apartment, lush markets, and a crowd of youthful entrepreneurs beneath flame-lit rooftop parties. Everything would be taken care of in Beijing. Most important, they'd be far from their families.

But their building's cracked pool and algae-covered water told a different story, as did the Silk Market, where dwindling tour groups bought imitation video watches and chopsticks lacquered with dragons. The holographic marketplace had moved on, and David and Gabriel were

tech refugees abandoned amid failing startups and the
fizzling promise of success. Nothing in China was free,
especially not the patching. But it was rumored that
somewhere in Nigeria, where the air was still breathable,
people stood on the tops of skyscrapers, sipping expensive drinks as DJs spun records until dawn, and Gabriel
wondered: Had they chosen Africa instead, would their
love have survived? Perhaps they could've found their
breath together. Maybe David would still be alive.

⁎

"You need to patch your family," David told him. It was
early evening, the six o'clock haze of Beijing heavy in
the apartment with a miniature ecosystem of beige and
brown strati. They were lying in bed, breathing slowly
without their tanks. Gabriel's head hurt from the previous night's partying, and whenever he ran his thoughts
over the memories of their fight, he could feel the rough
edges.

"I'm not patching my parents."

"Why the fuck not? I've been happy since I did it."

Gabriel wasn't sure this was true. David had been
filling in too much, his mind becoming a patchwork of
threadbare synapses that no longer held the memory
of their first kiss. And sure, David's parents were worthy
of patching—a father who'd regularly left him bloodied,
and a mother who'd prayed over him afterward—but by
filling those awful memories, David had removed *their*
history.

"Don't you miss our memories?" Gabriel asked.

"What are you worried about? I've got you right here, we can make new memories," David said. Gabriel fidgeted with the fabric of the bedsheets, and David reached down to take his hand. "What is it?"

"You used to know what it was like to lose your family. We talked about your dad—"

"*Stop,*" David said. "I patched him for a reason."

"Well, maybe you don't need to process anymore, but I do. Can't you remember anything about Bloomington? How you held me when I cried?"

"Honestly, no. We just cried about the past together?" Gabriel nodded. "Isn't that what depressed people do?"

"No, David, it's what real people do."

"Well, another thing *real people* do is patch. I know you keep hoping your family's going to change, but they're not. It's been three years since you heard from them. You've got to stop picking at those scabs. Come on," David said, placing his hand on Gabriel's heart. "It's time to get your memories filled."

It sounded so easy. And the truth was, Gabriel chewed on bad memories daily and they festered within him, filling even good times with despair. Like his final Christmas at home, the snowstorm, his brother's grip against his head as he'd held his face in the snow. How he'd walked all the way to an open Denny's where he'd called a boy he knew from college, who drove two hours to bring him to the safety of a warm apartment that holiday season.

"I'm glad you feel happier," Gabriel finally said, "and

I wouldn't wish your pain on anyone, but I don't want to be patch-happy."

David removed his hand from Gabriel's heart. He sat up in bed, inhaling slowly, trying to find a good breath. "Wow," he said, reaching for his clothes. "I think I finally get it. You *liked* that I was suffering."

"*What?*"

David put on his boxers. "As long as I didn't heal, you never had to. That's why you want me to cry with you. But I'm sorry, I don't want to do that, it's not who I am anymore. I'm healed and you're bringing me down."

"You're not healed, you're lying to yourself."

"*Actually,*" David said, and the word had never sounded so ugly, "I'm lying every time I say I love you." Then he rose from Gabriel's reach, and Gabriel didn't try to hold him back. Instead, he rolled over and listened to the apartment door shutting as David left for another club, a place where a fellow partyer, who'd had every neural pathway filled except his self-hatred, opened fire on the crowd before turning the gun on himself.

A surgeon in Beijing had said he could fill the memories of David for five thousand yuan. He wasn't a party neurosurgeon, just an old man with a dingy office near Tiananmen Square. The surgeon could keep their first kiss and David's warm touch, but all their Beijing life—their fights, and the memory of identifying David's body—those, the surgeon would fill like cavities. Gabriel had the man's card back at the apartment. What would be so wrong with patching the memories of how David had wasted all their money and broken his heart, Gabriel wondered, as he walked toward his brother's hotel.

Shanghai had more working air stations than Beijing, especially along the river where tourists and businessmen strolled, and he took this route past the Ionic columns and marble façades that made the Riverwalk resemble the palaces of a long-ago European empire. The outlines of plum blossoms, pockmarked with sand, materialized from the haze along the walkway, their bark flaking like peeling skin, and there was a faint outline of the Yangtze River where huge shipping boats honked at one another as they cut through the foggy daylight.

His brother's hotel welcomed him with an oxygen-rich lobby scented by jasmine blossoms and, above him, invisible speakers played soft notes of a Nirvana song plucked from a Chinese harp. His brother had said to meet him in the dining room, and the concierge directed him to the large banquet hall where chefs prepared plates of dragon fruit and sautéed king shrimp. There, at a far table, was his brother, looking as large and foreboding as Gabriel remembered him.

"Gabe!" his brother said. And though Gabriel had told himself he'd never again allow his brother to touch him, he met his brother's extended hand with his own. "You look tired," his brother said. "You tired?"

"Not really," Gabriel lied.

"Well, take a seat, I've ordered us dumplings and a bunch of dishes I can't pronounce. Figured you'd be hungry." Jake looked well fed, tanned, and relaxed, like a man who had regular access to oxygen. "Want something to drink? Company's paying for it." He waved over the waiter. "What are you having?"

"Water."

"Just water?" Jake asked. "I'll have your best *baijiu* and some jasmine tea; just water for my little brother." He waited for the waiter to leave before turning back to Gabriel. "So, three years—wish I could say you look happy, but you don't. You doing okay?"

Gabriel risked a truth. "Beijing's been awful." And his brother did something Gabriel had never known him to do: he listened. So Gabriel told him more. How trying to breathe at night left his lungs feeling bruised. How sometimes he thought he'd do anything for the price of a one-way ticket home where the sky was still blue. When he got to the part about crawling across his apartment because the only breathable air was by the floor, his brother folded his hands in a prayer-like way that reminded Gabriel of their father.

"I'm really sorry you've had such a rough time," Jake said. "What about the job?"

"It wasn't what it promised."

"Sounded like a scam when you told me about it. Well, good news is, I'm here to bring you home. Mom's not doing well. She got depressed and started being afraid of leaving the house after you left—"

"*Left?* Mom and Dad kicked me out."

"Gabe, you're the one who needed to reach out. Mom and Dad have always been willing to take you back. You only had to go to therapy, not China."

Gabriel focused on the tablecloth, where the silverware shone brightly and the water was as crystal pure as the air. He wondered what would happen if he knocked the glass over. Would his brother be able to move fast enough before it ruined his suit? The waiter placed a hot cup of jasmine tea in front of his brother along with the baijiu before retreating to leave the men alone.

"Listen, Mom had a nervous breakdown last month, she's been in the hospital, they're afraid she's suicidal. Dad needs your help, and I can't move from Miami with the kids and Trish. I talked to Dad, he's willing to make room for you at the Indy branch, said if you prove yourself with a starting-level position there's room for promotion. Plus, they have that apartment they never use. I know you're not interested in the business, but look at me, I'm living a good life while you're struggling to breathe. Come home and stay there until you get on your feet. Seriously, it sounds like you're living a nightmare. Are you even still with that guy?"

"No."

"See, you might as well come back to Indiana. All you

have to do is lie. Tell Mom and Dad you've changed. Mom needs to hear that. You know you're hurting her, right?"

"*Hurting her?* She locked me out in a blizzard. You held my face in a snowbank and nearly killed me. I could've died and she—"

"Fuck." His brother let out a long, slow whistle and unclasped his hands. He rested his fists on the white linen. "You're still going to hold on to that? Even though Mom's a wreck?"

Gabriel was silent. Around the dining room, the other guests seemed happy. A twentysomething-year-old girl picked at the roast duck on her plate and dipped it in hoisin sauce as she scrolled through her phone. There was the sound of people laughing at a far table, the rattle of waiters clearing dishes, and above it all, a Chinese harp version of "Girls Just Want to Have Fun."

His brother took a long breath and let his fists unclench. "Listen," he said. "The doctors have recommended Mom patch. Pastor Dan agrees, says it's the only way to move forward."

"Fine, let Mom patch."

"You don't get it. Mom's going to patch *you*," Jake said. And suddenly, the room was filled with too much air for Gabriel to breathe. "Dad's going to patch, too. Says it'll be easier to forget you than lie to Mom. You'll be gone from this family with no way of coming back. They wanted to fill you last week, but I stopped them. I said I'd heard from you, that you'd changed, that I was going to bring you back."

A thousand futures opened around Gabriel, each with its own destiny. In one, he picked up the cup and threw the steaming jasmine tea in his brother's face; in another, he grabbed the chopsticks and used them to gouge out Jake's eyes; and in another, he whispered, *"Okay,"* and became one of the many boys he'd seen in Beijing, the Chinese sons about to be disowned from real-estate money who'd danced with abandon beneath the blue lights of the club and a year later could be found scratching their patched scalps as they rented shitty apartments to couples in the outskirts of Beijing. They were ghostly replicas of themselves, now with wives or fiancées: patched men who Gabriel knew would still get hard if he kissed them. Gabriel also saw his own future: his entire life's history replaced with surgeon's spackle, worship songs, and the love of a family who would otherwise have patched him.

"Do you understand what I'm telling you?"

"Yeah," Gabriel finally answered. "David was right, I should've patched Mom and Dad a long time ago."

"Dude, what's wrong with you? You look like you're fucking dying here. Come home. I'll buy you the ticket. Just lie to Mom and Dad. They aren't monsters; they love you."

"Are you going to patch me, too?"

"I'm not going to patch my own fucking brother," Jake said. "But they will."

Gabriel rose from his seat and put his napkin on the table. "Well, then I guess you'll be the one to lie to them for the rest of your life."

"Gabe, *stop*—"

For a moment, it seemed like Jake would rise and tackle him to the ground as he'd done that Christmas, but he didn't. Instead, Gabriel crossed the banquet hall, out into the lobby with its scented air and its glass dispensers of iced water, and walked through the spiraling doors into the city with its thick, unbreathable air.

Gabriel tried not to think about David, or his brother, or his parents as he walked through the fog. What was left for him in Beijing? Clothes perpetually stained by smog, smoky sheets, dishes spotted with soap drying on a dish towel by the sink, and yes, photos of David, but otherwise nothing he needed to return to. The only place he could think of going now was the temple they'd once planned to visit. He placed the mask of an air station over his mouth and inhaled deeply. There was no stench of urine, only the musty smell of other users' breaths, and he stood there inhaling as he scrolled for directions to Longhua Temple. *Breathe,* he told himself, before continuing toward the subway station and onto a train which rocked passengers back and forth as they held on to the overhead rail, trying to compete for air.

Longhua station was filled with destruction. Around the old temple, jackhammers tore up the road and the buildings had been reduced to rubble. There were rusted I-beams, scaffolding, and plywood fences hastily erected. Amid all this stood the small enclosed oasis of the old

Buddhist temple. Gabriel paid the entry fee and accepted the two sticks of incense from the attendant. There were pyres within the courtyard, filled with the ashes of previous visitors' prayers, and he placed his incense by the smoldering sticks in the burning well where all blessings were delivered. What prayers did he have anymore? What blessings?

Along the awnings of the pavilions, a hundred red paper lanterns swung in the smog that blew through the monastery. Gabriel searched the courtyard for a Bodhi tree but found only open temple doors. Within the first building was a shrine of the Buddha, the enormous golden statue sitting serenely. In another was Guan Yin, the Bodhisattva of Compassion, with her thousand hands, an eye within each palm. And in yet another, the Gods of the Four Directions guarded a ceiling painted with an infinite lotus flower, a vision of the spiraling universe glimpsed upon death. All of it was too enormous for Gabriel, too otherworldly, and he stepped with confusion through a room that housed five hundred golden statues of Buddha, their faces full of mirth.

The final courtyard was thick with smoke and there were no Bodhi trees left, only monks in saffron robes making their way past the temples to a small room in one of the longhouses at the back of the pavilion. They sat around a wooden table, their air tanks behind them, and the rhythm of their movements was like a flock of starlings in murmuration. Their hands cycled up and down, lifting their masks to their noses, so that while some inhaled, others exhaled their prayers. A gong sounded from the small building, echoing into the dusty temple grounds, and then, like the humming of a thousand song-birds, the monks' chanting rose from within the room. The sound caught Gabriel so unexpectedly that the wind left him, and he fell to his knees by the open doorway, fighting to catch his breath among the fumes.

Once, a long time ago, sandstorms blew smog past their windows like otherworldly clouds. David had taken him into his arms, and Gabriel had listened to the hum of his voice as David promised them a new life together. Now, everything he loved was gone: David was dead, his family forever inaccessible, the plane tickets to the US null and void. He was on his own, with nothing left but his breath, which seemed impossible to find amid the plastic fumes.

Alone at this monastery, where all was peaceful and every statue promised enlightenment, Gabriel felt the tears coming. They rolled down his face as the monks continued their polyphonic chanting beneath their oxygen masks, one voice layering atop the next, and he closed his eyes and let his tears fall. He didn't open them when he felt the robes of the monk by his side, didn't wipe his tears when the mask was placed over his nose and mouth. He just listened to the chanting, the music washing through the courtyard like waves of an incoming tide, and took his first breath.

COMFORT PORN

The wind on the water is strong enough to create waves, and the sun casts the scene in early summer light. When the camera pans away from the ocean and up onto the beach, there's a crew of friends having a BBQ. The girls in bikinis wave, and the guys wearing cargo shorts and linen button-downs raise their beer bottles in my direction. One guy—bearded, tattooed, and standing alone—turns and looks at the camera.

"Hey, Mandy," he says through my laptop speakers. Warmth spreads across my chest. The other friends turn to face the screen, their voices full of laughter. "Hey, you! Get over here! We've been waiting for you!"

Click. Pause. Drag the time bar thirty seconds earlier. Play.

Bearded-tattooed guy turns, his sandy hair blowing in the wind.

"Hey, Mandy," he says. The others turn to face the camera, and my heart swells, pushing forward my tears. "Get over here! We've been waiting for you!"

Pause. Reverse. Play.

"We've been waiting for you!"

Pause. Reverse. Play.

"We've been waiting for you!"

And I'm crying now, my cheeks wet, my heart wide open. I take a tissue, dab my eyes, and let it drop to the floor. Then I click out of the window, shut down my computer, and get up to start the night.

Sometimes I watch hardcore clips. Dance raves where a friend leads the camera through group after group of partiers—dozens of people facing the screen and waving as I pass. "Oh, my god, Mandy! You look so good!" a pretty girl says. Other times I choose romance clips, the ones with the deep murmur of a man's voice calling to me from the bedroom. The camera turns a corner, I see the flicker of candles, the white of his smile, feel the sudden expansion of my heart and the warm wash of being wanted.

There are baby showers, birthday parties, and clips that are nothing more than a lopsided drunken night at a bar with someone off camera yelling, "You're so fucking funny!" Mostly, though, I watch friendship clips: A group on a baseball field in midsummer. A Frisbee tossed. A girl in cutoffs drinking a beer. The quintessential mid-July day with the sun falling and a grill lit in the background.

The guy throwing the Frisbee turns and faces the camera. "Hey, you made it." Then the other players turn. "Look, everyone, Mandy's here!" The girl in cut-offs waves; the guy tending the grill raises his bottle in welcome.

And everyone is so happy to see me.

After I'm done watching comfort porn, I eat dinner and flip through Firestarter on my phone. There's a photo of an iPhone-lit penis, the shot most guys use for their profile. I trash the pic. The next guy is surrounded by two kids. Trash. Five more dick pics. Trash. A guy with two douchey-looking dudes on either side of him and "Gang-bang!" written across their chests. Trash. There's a hot thirty-year-old at a pool party. Either the photo's staged or it's spam—no one goes to actual pool parties anymore. Still, he's standing by a grill and laughing. Maybe he has real friends. I swipe right and the match ignites immediately.

Hey, girl! Lol. Had to get off this app. SO BORING! Check out my private photos at—

Trash.

I send two other guys a fire emoji but no spark, and finally I see a semi-decent-looking guy who's kind of hot in one of his pics. He's only rated three out of five campfires by past dates but has an 86% safety-and-consent rating from more than seventy-five users. He likes doggy-style and anal, and he prefers girls who squirt. Not ideal, but I still swipe right. My fire ignites with an immediate flame.

Hey, he messages. *You're hot. Free tonight?*

Yup.

Cool, let's hook up.

OK. But my place and you pay for Uber.

Deal.

I send him a winking/kissy face with a heart on the lips. He sends one back and my phone dings: *Permit address share?* I click Yes, get an image of a crackling fireplace and the message *Have a Fiery Night!* Since Uber arrival isn't for another twenty minutes, I clean up the bedroom, throw dirty clothes into the hamper, and finally sit on the couch drinking a beer and scrolling through Firestarter until he buzzes.

He's heavier than the photos he's shared.

"Hey, you," he says, trying to sound sexy. His lips curl slightly at the edges when he smiles, and there's something almost like attraction.

"Hi."

"You're shorter than your photos."

"I rounded up," I admit.

"That's cool. I have to work early. Okay if we just fuck?"

"Sure, let's do the couch."

As much as I hate ForPlay, it does help guys with fin-

gering. Men are always stroking their phones on the subway, listening to some female-app voice moan in their
earbuds as they practice techniques. Clearly it's helped
this guy. He gets me off while kissing my neck and whis-
pering, "You're awesome." Then he wants to do anal, even
though my profile specifically states I don't do that on first
dates. I remind him about that, and he says it's a letdown
but if I'm up for swallowing, he'll be happy enough. So I
get him off like he wants and he gets dressed.

"Thanks," he says. "I'll give you a positive rating."

"I'll do the same," I lie.

After he's gone, I log back onto the computer and pull
up private browsing to search for a cozy clip. There's a
whole bunch of hiking clips, a winter skiing vacation with
friends, and a surprise birthday party that usually makes
me happy. But none of those work tonight. I finally find
a holiday scene with wrapped presents and a handsome
man sitting cross-legged by a Christmas tree.

"Hey, Mandy!" he says to the camera, holding his arms
out wide. "Come sit by me." And I feel the sudden expansion of my heart, the tears arriving right on cue.

Pause. Reverse. Play.

Pause. Reverse. Play.

Pause. Reverse. Play.

When I moved to New York, I thought I'd get an apartment in Bushwick where all the artists lived, but it turned
out everything there was too expensive. I ended up in

Dyker Heights, in a fourth-floor efficiency with no air-conditioning and no space to work on my art. I'd hoped the city would be inspiring, but the only available job was a part-time gig doing window design in downtown Manhattan. It was a two-hour commute for a three-hour job, and I'd return every night depressed from seeing so many people who looked like they'd given up. So I quit the job, made my apartment my island of safety, and started doing online profile edits.

During that time, I found some solace in Live Online Parties. Someone on Blogger would say they were hosting a party, I'd pay the streaming cover, and people would talk to the camera like they were my friends. They'd smile a lot and say all the right things, and everyone would act excited and wave when the camera passed, but it felt phony. The pillows on the couches were always fluffed in the right way, the lights around the kitchen were twinkly like in Snapshot posts, and some dumb stranger would throw their arms toward the screen like they were my old friend and get my name wrong. I always ended up leaving the site after an hour to watch comfort porn, where at least the acting was better.

Eventually I joined Hang-Out, which seems like a good way to stay social. It's $9.99 a month and though it feels like you're paying for friends, Hang-Out reminds you that you're only paying for the service, not the people. *We'll never charge you for extra friends*, they say, which is a good motto, except you can't access any personal messages that members send unless you pay the extra monthly fee. But

I figured it was worth the cost. I read an article that said five minutes of actual social interaction is good for the lymphatic system.

There's a group called Board Game Night. Every Thursday, people looking for friends get together in Astoria to drink micro-distilled whisky and play retro games like Monopoly and Sorry. I went a couple times, but everyone was trying to be buddy-buddy and overdoing it. They yelled "Oh my god!" when all I was doing was moving my car past Go. People were friendly and they pretended to like one another, but nobody asked for my number, so I joined a Volleyball Hang-Out instead to get exercise along with the social interaction.

This week's Hangout is at Rockaway Beach, and by the time I arrive there's twenty-something people socializing around a volleyball net, looking exactly like a comfort porn clip. There's a grill, but no one remembered to bring charcoal, so there's just a cooler full of iced hot dogs and cold beer. Down at the shoreline, a girl wearing a batik wraparound dances wild and free. She strips the tapestry off her waist and lifts it above her head, letting it whip in the wind as she moves, and I wish I could look that spontaneous and seductive, even if it's just for a selfie promo clip—which it is: She's got a tripod set up. It'll be uploaded on Hang-Out and get a thousand Firestarter invites by this afternoon.

"Hey, you!" five guys say in unison as I approach.

"Want a beer?" a dude in a screen-printed Buddha tee asks.

"Sure. Thanks!"

He pops the cap and hands it to me. "I'm Jeff." We shake hands, his palm cold from the bottle, and he motions to the volleyball court. "You play?"

"I did in high school."

"Good enough for me. You can be on our team." He gives me a blue armband. "We're up after orange is done."

I meet some of the other players. A girl named Shawna, two brothers, Jack and Tom, who run a DIY charcuterie business in Hoboken, and a forty-nine-year-old woman named Destiny who leads virtual-reality Kabbalah workshops. The purple team ends up winning, so we take our positions against them. Our team isn't great. Most of our players are more interested in getting photos of themselves than actually playing. They give one another high fives every single time we score, and I have to wait for them to take a bunch of selfies together. When I dive to save a spike, the charcuterie brothers go way overboard, telling me that was the sickest shit they've ever seen, but Jeff is cool. He just gives me a thumbs-up, so perfect it's almost straight out of a comfort porn clip, and I feel my cheeks flush.

After our team loses, the Hangout starts to break up. Someone says they can go get charcoal, but you can tell everyone just wants to go home. It's already been an awkward hour with a bunch of strangers. Destiny says goodbye with too much emotion and gives everyone hugs, and the selfie girl slinks off with one of the charcuterie brothers.

"Nice playing," Jeff says as I get my bag.

"Thanks—beginner's luck."

"You interested in seeing Bottle Beach?"

"What's that?"

"There's an old factory that busted open down the road and there's Prohibition glass everywhere—old bottles, marbles, pottery scraps, all washed up. It's pretty apocalyptic. I could show you if you've got good shoes?"

"Sneakers."

"That'll work."

And though I know this is how people get killed, I say okay, because it's the first time a guy has invited me anywhere in years. I drive us to the parking lot near Dead Horse Bay, and we walk down an overgrown trail full of summer lilies and wild blackberries until we arrive on one of the most unromantic beaches I've ever seen. The beach is completely covered with broken pottery, old tiles, and medicine bottles glistening in the afternoon sun. There's barely anywhere to walk without stepping on shattered glass. A couple of seagulls stalk clumsily through the shards, pecking at debris to uncover clamshells.

"Wow, this is so fucked up."

"Check it out, a whole one." Jeff holds up a purple medicine bottle and extends it to me. "Want it?"

"Really?"

"Yeah, I have a dozen at home. I've been here before."

"Thank you, I love it," I say, because even though getting a sandy, sludge-filled medicine bottle on a beach of broken glass isn't a comfort porn clip, it feels close. So I take a risk, lean in, and kiss his cheek.

"That was nice," he says, and when he asks me what I'm doing for dinner, I can't help but feel like I'm in a movie.

We go to a Korean place that specializes in early-aught decor. There's lots of Ikea furniture from my parents' generation, and the patio has REI camping chairs and a Bluetooth speaker playing Modest Mouse from a weathered iPod. Our server wears Old Navy clothes and takes our order. She's nice and winks at me, and I try to remember the last time I was on a date rather than a Firestarter hookup.

"This place is great," I say after she's left. "I can't believe they have an internet café!"

"I know, right? It's hysterical."

"So . . . ," I say, "can I ask you a personal question?"

"Sure."

"Are you on Firestarter?"

"Closed down my account months ago. Probably stupid since everyone is on it, but I wanted to see what meeting people in real life felt like."

"How's *that* working out for you?"

"Pretty awesome. I'm here with you, right?"

And I want to kiss him right then. Instead I just say, "Totally," and the server brings us our *soju*.

Jeff tells me about his gig selling Buddhist screen-prints to yoga studios, and I tell him about my freelance job editing Aphrodite profiles. "It's mostly just for aging millennials who think sex is more dignified if you post rambling descriptions of yourself and go on old-fashioned dates."

"Like we're doing?"

"This is a real date." I point my finger at him. "Aphrodite's for people who need the justification of dinner to fuck. They eat together, have phony-deep conversations, then hook up and never message one another again, exactly as if they were on Firestarter."

Jeff reaches across the table and takes my hands. "I like that we met in real life." And though I know I'm blushing, I look up and tell him I like it, too.

I invite Jeff back to my place, which feels risky. It's the kind of thing all the blogs tell you never to do. I have no clue what his ratings are or if he's been preapproved for safety and consent, but at my door he takes my hand before I get out my keys. "I know you haven't seen my profile or anything," he says, "but you should know I had a ninety-five percent on Firestarter. I can reactivate my account or give you access to past relationships if you'd like."

I want to tell him he's perfect in that moment, but instead I just kiss him. And then we're inside my apartment, pulling off each other's clothes and wrapping our arms around each other on my bed. He holds me close, his breath against my neck as we fuck, and after it's over he kisses me, which is something guys never do once they've come. When he asks if I want him to sleep over, my eyes wince and I feel warmth spread across my chest.

There's this clip I used to watch. On-screen you see

darkness, then a brief fluttering of light, and finally the camera's eye flickers open, blinking in the soft morning sunlight. There's a cute guy, his close-shaven face looking at the camera. "Hey, babe," he says. "Want some coffee?" It was always that moment which made me tear up, and I want Jeff to stay and drink coffee with me in the morning, but then I worry he'll just be like the last dude. A guy who didn't ask if I wanted coffee, only asked whether we could do anal since it was technically the second date.

"You don't have to stay," I tell him. "I'm just going to fall asleep. Besides, I have lots of profile edits to do in the morning."

"Maybe next time, then," he says, and kisses me again. He finds his boxers and puts them on, searches for his pants where we stripped them, and locates his socks and shirt. I wrap the blanket around me and walk him to the door, feeling cozy. The light from the hallway highlights his face, and he doesn't just leave like Firestarter guys, but turns and gives me a deep kiss in the doorway.

"Text me tomorrow," I tell him.

"I will," he says.

And then he's gone.

I wake up groggy and alone and get started on Aphrodite edits. There's a woman who's over forty but has a hot face. She wants to know why she can't get a date.

"Delete *Not looking for drama*," I tell her. "Only people

with drama write that. Get rid of angry-cat coffee mug photo. Do you have any kissy-lip pics to make you look younger?" I edit her profile photos to perfection, dodge and burn contour lines, tint and brighten her body, add glimmer to eyes and thickness to lips, and create a selfie that will change her life from Cupid-less to so many hits she couldn't date them all if she wanted.

My next client's a dude in Michigan who's shirtless and holding up a string of fish. He's asking me for literary references that'll *land a smart/successful woman*. "Fishing pic DOES NOT send the message of smart/successful. Makes you look redneck. Take a selfie at sunset with a stack of books on patio table. Talk about farm-to-table dining (see attached video)."

It feels good to help people out, like one way my art degree hasn't been a complete waste, and it pays the rent every month and enough for a diet of fruit and yogurt. For a while I told myself I'd start painting again—bump it up to one hundred and forty profiles a day, put in an eighty-hour workweek, enough to buy new brushes and canvases—but I gave up after two years. Seventy profiles a day is my max, and today I'm lagging because of the heat. Last summer there were suggested evacuations and I should've moved out of my apartment. Instead, I filled two casserole dishes with ice to put my feet in and sweated through the hundred-and-twenty-degree days.

By noon, I've got the ice baths back out and I'm dripping sweat on my keyboard. Jeff still hasn't messaged me.

To distract myself, I scroll through Hang-Out posts. It's mostly photos of people getting drunk; another selfie video of the batik girl from the beach doing yoga on a rooftop; and a post from someone I met at Game Night who's getting rid of her AC. It's huge and free, but I have to transport it myself, and there's no way I can carry that thing alone. I imagine me and Jeff getting it together like we're in a romance clip. He's making silly jokes as he helps carry it up my four flights of stairs. After we install it, we get pizza and a six-pack of IPA, and we sit in our sweaty T-shirts in the late-afternoon sun, beads of sweat condensing against our bottles. And though I know it's stupid to message him the idea, I also figure: Why not? He's retro. It'd be kinda romantic and old-fashioned.

"Hey U!" I type. "Soooo . . . any chance you want to help me move an air conditioner? I'll treat to pizza and beer afterward." I read the message five times, get rid of the ellipsis, then put it back, add an exclamation mark, then remove it, change the smiley emoji to a kissy-face, then a winky-face, then back to a smile. Finally I take a deep breath and hit Send. I wait. There're no ellipses of him responding. Not after one minute. Not after five. Not after ten. The only incoming messages are from Fire-starter dudes asking if I want to do doggy-style. So I go back to profile edits and try to forget that I sent such a stupid, needy message.

At six, I take a break, order Indonesian, and ignore my silent phone. I click over to Hang-Out. The air conditioner's still there, with a couple of comments. *Looks Cool—haha!* Someone else posted a snowflake emoji next to a hot flame. *I'll heat you up. Check out my profile on Firestarter.* I scroll through my emails as I eat dinner, opening and deleting messages, trying to feel nostalgic by remembering what it was like when people still took the time to write emails. There's a bunch from my parents, dated last year—they're writing about how beautiful Ohio autumn is and sending Christmas greetings; a thousand spam emails and Uber receipts which I trash; and a strange email with the subject "NYC Visit?"

> Amanda! It's Katie! Can you believe it's been twelve years since art school? Tried to call and message you but don't think you have the same number. Figured I'd email as a last shot. Thinking about you! Remember that sunset painting you made? I still have it (!!!) Are you in NYC? I'm in Ithaca, would be great to come visit you and the city! Could really use friend time. Miss you! —Katie :)

I read over the email again. Then I check the date. She sent it six months ago. *Visit? Friend time?* Is she joking? Who asks something like that? I live in an efficiency and, sure, there's room for her to crash on the floor, but if she wants to not pay me for an Airbnb stay that's just plain rude. Besides, who sends long rambling messages full of punctuation marks like they're in Y2K? I wonder if this is a new scam and her account's been hacked.

My phone pings with a message from Jeff.

AC? Sorry, not looking for that kind of commitment. Wishing you best of luck! Stay off Firestarter! Haha! Then there's a pause, the soft ebb of ellipses. I'm waiting for him to type *JK! Would love to!* with a laughing-so-hard-I'm-crying emoji, but it's just a cartoon peace sign.

Okay, fuck him. Just another guy who learned the tricks of comfort porn to pick up women as desperate as me. I'm so mad that I click back over to Katie's email and tell her it's super creepy for her to ask to *visit,* and if she's actually gung-ho to see me and not just some scammer asshole . . .

I pause over the keys. The truth is I do remember the painting of the sunset. I made it while we sat on a hill near the edge of campus, passing a joint back and forth. I'd told her I wanted to move to New York City and change the world with my art, and Katie had said she knew I could do it, was sure I'd be famous one day.

I read what I wrote, backspace, and start typing again. If she's not a scammer, I tell her, I could use help moving an AC, and in exchange will let her crash for the night. Then, before I can second-guess myself, I hit Send, thinking I probably just fell for a really dumb hoax. But two hours later my inbox dings with her reply. *Haha! Not a scammer :) Happy to help ya move that sucka AC!* It's a really long email, asking me loads of personal questions and telling me how much she's missed me. The last line of the email is *Love you, friend,* with an old-school punctuation-mark smiley-face. And I don't know why the word *friend* or that stupid punctuation smile makes me want to cry, but it does.

Katie was hot in college, which is why when I open the door I think she must be a neighbor I don't know. She's gained at least sixty pounds, and her clothes are down-right frumpy; she wouldn't get a single campfire on Fire-starter. But she's all smiles, and she takes me into her arms when I see her.

"Mandy!" she says. "You look so good!"

"And you look—"

"Plump and happy. No need to lie, it's God's truth. I can't believe it's been twelve years. Hey, I remember that poster!" She points at the Paris stock print of a black cat, tall and lanky, its tail curled around a cappuccino. I'd bought it at a college sale and hung it in my dorm because it felt sophisticated. When I moved to NYC I took it with me because I thought it made me seem artsy. I look at the curled corners of the poster with Fun-Tak grease stains. Just a dumb print I got at a dumb college poster sale.

"I'm thinking of getting rid of it."

"Really? I'll take it! I remember smoking joints with you and spacing on it."

"Come on in," I say. "Can I get you a drink?"

"Water would be good," Katie says, putting down her backpack. "It's hot as hell in here, you need an air condi-tioner!" She laughs and sits in my bird's-nest chair, and I bring her the glass of water. The only other place to sit in the room is at the small kitchen table or on my bed, so I decide to sit on the carpet facing her.

"Pretty crazy to be back together, isn't it?" she says.

It is. I want to tell her this isn't something people do, just go and visit each other after twelve years, but instead I ask what she's been up to.

"It's been a roller coaster since college," she says, sipping her water. "But you don't want to hear about that."

I don't, but I say I do.

"Well, I moved to San Fran like I said I would, thinking it'd be a cool art scene—except there're no artists there anymore, just app designers and holograph-tech dudes, and rent was five K a month for an efficiency. I tried to make it work, but the city literally stank with fallout from the spill. Dead fish were washing up, and the wildfires made everything smell like rotten smoked salmon. It was like living in an expensive apocalypse where everyone's dying slowly but drinking cold-brewed nitro lattes. I didn't make any art, just worked a shitty job. So I finally applied for my MFA and got into Ohio."

"You moved back to the Midwest?"

"I know. But Columbus was an okay place. I met a guy named Eric in the program, and when we graduated he got an offer at Cornell, so we moved upstate and I started adjuncting art classes. Then he proposed and we bought a house—"

"Oh my god, congratulations!"

"Well, that wedding never happened. A month after he proposed, I started getting awful headaches and was gaining all this weight and having weird nerve spasms. Finally the doctor sends me to get an MRI—and that's when they found the tumor." She points to her head.

"What?"

"Size of a golf ball. Meanwhile, I'm getting sicker and sicker and bigger and bigger, and that's when Eric decides a lifelong commitment given my diagnosis was too heavy. 'How about a commitment to be here next fucking week?' I ask him. Too heavy. *Heavy's* the key word. Meanwhile I was, like, vomiting. So he left me with the mortgage, no health insurance or sick leave from my job. Everything pretty much went to hell after that. I lost the house, lost my savings, my parents had to sell their place to help with the cost of treatments."

I have a dim recollection of some posts she'd written about being sick, but I'd thought it was the flu. "I'm so sorry, I had no clue you were going through that."

Katie's flinch is almost unnoticeable, just a trace of sadness beneath her face. "Well, I got off social media after I got sick. It was mostly just photos of me in hospitals anyway—and no one was liking those. I tried calling you a bunch, I left messages—that must've been two or three years ago—but I guess you got a new number. I was in a pretty bad place, I was just so lonely. My parents were the only support I had left."

And it's right then that I realize what a mistake it was to invite Katie into my apartment. The long tragedy story, the subtle but effective guilt trip—it's a by-the-book setup. Soon she's going to ask for money.

"The doctors said I had a one-in-fifteen chance of living, but look, here I am! Cancer-free for two years. Haven't lost the weight, but honestly, it's freeing. At least I won't end up with another dickhead who's only with me for my looks. And you know, even in the darkest moments, there's hope. I'm adjuncting again, making interest payments on the medical bills, and I've met a nice guy." She takes out her phone and shows me a picture. The man's no winner. He's round like her and balding. They're standing in a pumpkin field, the sky behind them vibrant blue, the fields deep brown, both of them looking happy.

"Pablo's a sweetheart. It's great to have someone in your corner, you know? We moved into an apartment together, with access to a yard and berry bushes—oh right, almost forgot, I brought you a present." She digs into her shoulder bag and hands me a small mason jar. "Jam from this summer's blueberry crop."

"Wow," I say, waiting for her to hit me up for money, but the silence just stretches between us. Finally she gives me a smile. This is when the pitch comes.

"I hope you like it," she says. "It's really delicious."

Even though I've got loads of profiles to edit, Katie wants to see Prospect Park, so we make our way there in her car. I do edits on my phone as she drives, but she keeps asking me questions about my life, bringing up memories from college, and reminding me of days filled with painting and late nights with jugs of wine and visions of a future better than this one. We used to throw parties with the art and dance majors, and every weekend I'd stalk off through our small college town in search of sunlight, buildings, and blue skies worth painting, figuring this was what life was going to be like, one long stretch of art and community. If I'd known who I'd become by the time I was twenty-nine, living alone in a crumbling NYC efficiency and editing profiles all day, I never would've believed it.

"You seriously don't paint anymore? You were a fantastic artist! I always thought you were just super busy being famous."

"No," I say, wishing she'd drop the subject.

"What about your canvases? Have you tried getting a gallery show?"

"Katie, no one's offering me a gallery show. There's no way you can live in this city and be an artist. I'm happy I left painting behind, it wasn't getting me anywhere."

"So move," she says, and I realize then that she liked the person I was in college way better than the person I am now.

"I'm fine," I say. "I love living in the city, and profile editing is a way of using my art degree for something that actually makes money." Firestarter dings with five potential flames in the area who are interested in having me blow them.

"Okay," she says. "You just seemed really happy when you were painting, is all."

I'm thankful when we finally find a parking spot and

can walk into the openness of the park. There's a couple of Hang-Out groups tossing Frisbees and drinking beers.

"Wow, it's beautiful here," Katie says as we sit on the grass. She looks around at the people sunbathing and a group of guys kicking a soccer ball back and forth. "I feel like I'd come here every day if I lived in the city."

"That's what I thought, too. I haven't been here in years." My phone dings. The three guys playing soccer want to gangbang me.

"Okay, seriously, what's up with your phone?"

"Firestarter," I say.

Katie's never heard of it, so I show her the app, tell her how easy it is to create a profile, explain how it could've helped her during her lonely period. "There's check boxes for everything from bondage to group sex," I tell her, but Katie doesn't reply, she's just scrolling through the men. "Most of the guys you're looking at spent their teenage years jerking off to facials, so you have to check that box or you just end up with a bunch of old dudes pretending to be gentlemanly. Sure enough, when they're ready to come, they all want facials!" I say, and laugh. I've given that monologue a dozen times at Hang-Out events, and whenever I do, the women will be cracking up or nodding their heads and telling me to preach. But Katie's just sitting there, looking at me like I told her I drowned a bag of kittens.

"*What?*" I finally ask.

She lifts the screen to show me a penis with a smiley face drawn on it in Sharpie. "This is what you do for a living? You edit *these?*"

"Not that site, it's another one called Aphrodite. I can show you."

"It's just . . ." She looks at the photo of the smiley-face penis again. "It's sick. I mean, can't you close down your account?"

"And do what? Talk to these guys?" I gesture to all the screen-cocked heads and thumb-typing sunbathers. "I'd have to ask them to take out their earbuds first."

"Mandy, you can't live like this."

"Like *what*?"

"Like choosing positions as if you're ordering pizza."

"Jeez," I say, taking back my phone. "I didn't realize you were so sex-shamey. This is how people date now. You've just been upstate making blueberry jam."

"I've been overcoming cancer."

"Well, you lost track of how things are. People don't talk and they don't date. They fuck and get on with their lives. Trust me, it's way easier that way."

"But this isn't how people are supposed to live. You need love. You need friendship."

"I have friends," I say, and I want to list off a dozen names to prove her wrong, but the only name I can come up with is Jeff's.

"Mandy," Katie reaches for my hands, "this wasn't why you wanted to move to New York. You wanted to make art, remember?"

"Yeah, I know, you keep reminding me of that. I got it, thanks, you think I suck now. Is that why you came to visit, to tell me my life is crap?"

"No, I came to see you because I missed you—"

"And what else? To ask for money? To get my old art? To sleep with me?"

"What are you talking about?"

"What do you want from me?"

"I don't want anything from you."

"That's not true—everyone wants things, it's the only reason anyone ever talks to you. They want sex, or connections, or free profile edits, and they only like you if they think they can get something."

"Mandy, I came because we used to be good friends. I know we haven't talked in years, but what you just said was *crazy*. We were really close, remember? And maybe I don't know how dating works, but I know that app sucks, and I know you need to take a break from this city. Come upstate. We have an extra room. You can work on profile edits there, too, right?"

"Yeah, but—"

"I'm talking a weekend. You need a getaway." She's still holding my hands in hers, like we're eight years old.

"Maybe," I admit.

She squeezes my hands before letting them go. "You want a hug?" And though I feel stupid, I tell her I do. So she scoots over and puts her arms around me, just the two of us holding each other like a bad comfort-porn clip, but it feels good, like when we used to paint together and stay up all night planning for a future where we'd be happy and famous.

"Now, didn't you say we have an air conditioner to

move?" Katie says, letting me go. "I mean, it's hot as fuck in your apartment."

So we drive across town and Katie parks illegally in front of an apartment building where a woman lives who I have listed as a friend on social media. The air conditioner is a beast, and our clothes get covered in old insulation foam as we wrestle the unit free from the window. We have to stop at least a dozen times on the way down the flights of stairs to catch our breath, Katie nearly tripping on the cord as she walks backward, all the while worrying that her car will be towed. It's a lot sweatier and messier than comfort porn and there's a whole lot more damns and ouches, and no cold beers, but it's also kind of fun—and when we get to the ground floor, her car isn't towed, just sitting there with its blinkers on. So we load the AC into her hatchback and drive across town, and then, in a moment that seems unbelievably perfect, we see an open spot in front of my apartment and actually high-five like we're in some super-old eighties film. Then we grunt as we haul the AC up my four flights until, finally, we slide it into the window, pull down and fasten the sash, and plug it in. When we turn it on, the unit hums with a gorgeous summer sound, cold air pouring from the coils, and we stand in the breeze, totally soaked with sweat.

"Jesus, fuck, good thing I didn't know what you were getting me into," Katie says. "You owe me a day of roto-tilling."

"Deal," I say. I look in the fridge for beers but there's just water and old apple juice.

"Water's good," Katie says. "I gotta head out soon any-way."

I'm by the sink filling her glass when I hear her say it. When she'd first emailed to tell me she was coming, I hadn't wanted her spending the night—there was no way I was giving up my bed, she could sleep on the floor with my camping mattress—but now I'd crash in the kitchen if she'd stay. I bring the water into the room.

"You're leaving?"

"Yeah. My kitty's gonna pitch a fit if I'm not back. I told you that in the email I sent. Oh, right, you don't check emails."

"But I have a bedroll I can use. Seriously, it's no prob-lem. You can totally have my bed for the night."

"Aw, honey, I wish I'd known you wanted me to stay. I didn't want to impose."

"But when are you leaving?"

"After I drink this water and sit for a minute in this lus-cious cold air. I really need to get back before midnight."

And suddenly it hits me just how much I do remember. How we'd dreamed about traveling to Germany together. How we were going to join an art house in Berlin, be rev-olutionaries, change the art world. And even though she's only been here for an afternoon, everything is imprinted with her—the bird chair where she sits, the jam jar on the counter, that stupid cat poster on the wall—and I can already feel how empty my apartment will be with-out her. The AC will be blowing cool air into the room, drowning out the noise of the street, and it'll be perfect and beautiful and exactly how I've always wanted my place to feel, and I know I can catch up on work, or try to find a guy on Firestarter, or cry over some good comfort porn, but I don't want any of those things.

"Don't go." The words tumble from my lips before I can stop them. Because in a moment I know I'll be washed under the tide of another seven years of this city, full of face after face of strangers, penis after penis, drowned by endless dick pics of men I don't know. "Please, don't go," I say again. And I'm not sure what exactly I'm asking for, only that I need her.

"Come here," she says, putting down her water. And this woman who I barely know anymore is pulling me close and placing her arms around me. And what do I do? I put my face into the softness of her shoulder and give in. I weep like a little kid as she puts her hand against my hair, holds me, and lets me cry. "Okay, let it all out," she says. And I do. I weep until everything in me is dry and she's warm and wet from my tears. She pulls some tissues out of her bag and hands them to me.

"I'm sorry," I say, and blow my nose.

"For what?"

"For, like, being a mess, and not being someone you can look up to anymore."

"Mandy, you're a good person. You just need friends. I do too, that's why I wanted to see you. And you need to get out of this city. Memorial Day is only a couple weeks away. You're visiting me, or I'm coming down and kidnapping you."

I look at her, sitting all sweaty in her frumpy shirt, beaming with goodness. "Why are you being so nice to me?"

"Because that's what friends do," she says. And though it sounds like the kind of thing you'd see on some dumb Hang-Out post, with a sepia-toned picture of two people clinking martinis, it also sounds like the truth. "You okay?" she asks, and I nod, though I'm not sure it's true. "Well, it's a long drive if I want to make it home before midnight. Next time let's move a couple fridges," she says, laughing. And then she's up, gathering her things, and I'm walking her down the sweltering staircase.

On the sidewalk, the final rays of sunshine make their way through the puzzle of buildings, lighting up the concrete in patches. I wrap my arms around Katie, feel her warmth against me, realizing all the options Firestarter has no checkboxes for: *Hugging. Holding. Staying.*

"Memorial Day, don't forget," she says. "And I know you only use your phone for bondage and threesomes, but I bet it works for calls, too." Then she's back in her car, pulling away from the curb, and I'm waving to her, actually waving as though I'm in a comfort porn video.

Across the street, a Hang-Out group is getting drunk at a bar, being loud and snapping photos of each other, and the outdoor tables are filled with coupled-up strangers. I see some of the people looking at me as I wave, but I don't care if they think I'm acting for a selfie video, it feels good. Ubers pass, each with a single rider or two heading elsewhere, on to their Aphrodite dates or back home from

Firestarter sessions. I continue to wave as Katie drives into the early evening. I'm waving even as she sits at the light waiting for it to turn green, my hand in the air as her car is swallowed by taxis, as though if I wave long enough, longer than I've ever seen in any comfort porn clip, this feeling will actually last.

(WE ONLY WANTED THEIR HAPPINESS)

We never should've opened our hearts to their tears. But how can you say no to your children? And when they asked why, we told them it was dangerous. They were only five, eight, ten; they were kids. Wasn't it enough that they had their smartphones? Their tablets? Their virtual reality consoles? Their screens upon screens upon screens?

But our children kept asking. Every birthday when they unwrapped their gifts of more electronics, we saw their disappointment. Why couldn't they have it? they asked over breakfast, over lunch, over dinner. They asked when we picked them up from school or went grocery shopping, and we spent hours repeating our reasons, only to be asked again when we tucked them into bed at night. Maybe, in retrospect, we agreed simply to get them to stop asking.

One could always have it removed, we reasoned. And we turned to our husbands and wives—our companions who should've stopped us—but they, too, were exhausted from all the pleading. Most days were spent checking texts with the compulsion of chain-smokers, or searching for funny memes as if seeking the Holy Grail. At the end of the day, all we wanted was a couple hours of uninterrupted scrolling.

And so we scheduled appointments for our children's birthdays. Or grandparents promised our kids the gifts. "We know it's expensive," our parents told us, "but we wanted to spoil them." And then what could we do? When our children heard the news, their faces were as joyous as if they'd been given a kitten.

The surgery was as painless as promised. A small handheld injector no larger than a pocket flashlight was pressed to our children's temples. "Count to three," the technician instructed. "One . . . two . . ." Our children winced, a couple tears appeared in the corners of their eyes, and then it was done. They opened their eyes, looking slightly dazed, and we took them out for ice cream, told them they'd been brave. At home we let them rest in bed, watched for symptoms, feared the worst. But they just lay in their dark rooms, their eyes shining, and finally they yawned, stretched their arms, and blinked on their inner connections.

They talked so much in those first weeks. We couldn't stop them. They talked upon waking, they talked in the shower, at breakfast, on the way to school, their small voices ringing out as if they were using their words for the last time. They narrated nonstop from backseats as they navigated the ether between their brains and our world, interacting with the animated animals that floated invisibly in the air. We grew tired of their ongoing laughter, their joy which excluded us. "Please," we said, "we just want a moment with you." "Ha!" they laughed, and told us they'd placed filters over our faces. We suddenly had giraffe ossicones, cat ears, and dog noses. "Hahaha!" Now we had horse teeth! Now fish lips! Speech bubbles emerged from our mouths when we told our kids to please turn off their browsers, it was time for dinner. "Hahaha!" They couldn't even hear what we were saying; they'd turned our voices into bird chirps! "Please," we asked them again, aware of the helplessness in our voices. "We need you to turn off your connections." And finally, they blinked and told us they had. But when they giggled during dinner, how could we be sure they'd closed anything down?

Then, all of a sudden, our children fell silent. We watched as they crouched in the middle of the carpet for hours—entertained by nothing, it seemed. They sat alone in their rooms, their hands building invisible castles. When we asked them once, twice, three times what they were doing, they told us with frustration to please be quiet: they were trying to concentrate. Our houses became silent again, and our children stopped asking for things. Only for our credit cards, which they needed to purchase upgrades. "No," we said. *"Please,"* they asked. "No," we repeated; we weren't about to put our credit card numbers into the ether. But they cried and they yelled at us, and when they wouldn't relent, we finally read the numbers and expiration dates off our cards.

We attempted to tell our children about the benefits of having some offline time. An hour or two, even a couple of minutes. Just to take a walk, to ride a bicycle, to play in the snow or watch springtime lightning storms. We printed up contracts with consequences for spending too long online, had our children sign on dotted lines, forced them to make promises that were never fulfilled. We begged. We pleaded. They told us they understood. Then they went back to their rooms to build invisible cities.

Their grades plummeted. All their homework was in the ether, and we watched them moving their hands in the air, looking no different than when they played online games. It sure didn't seem like math, but how could we check? We petitioned the school, wrote letters to the board of education, and launched isolated but vocal resistance at PTA meetings. Online education was fine, we said, but could we go back to tablets and laptops? We were patiently listened to by kindly educators who all nodded their implanted heads. They smiled at us with illuminated eyes and shared the good news: Our school's STEM program had just received a grant for low-income implantation. Philanthropically minded tech foundations would be offering free online textbooks; soon our district would be completely implanted, the libraries of the world as accessible to our children's brains as the back of their eyes.

Why didn't anyone understand? Our children needed sleep. Late at night, they lay in the darkness of their bedrooms wide-eyed and grinning. "Go to sleep," we told them. They needed rest. They were children. And yet, were they? Their minds now accessed every history lesson, every blog, every Googled answer to any argument we had. They'd long ago surpassed us. "Go to sleep!" we yelled, and immediately felt horrible about our parenting. Later, we'd peek into their rooms, see their closed eyes, their faces reminding us of the toddlers we once knew, and we'd sigh with relief. Yet how could we ever be sure they were sleeping?

We decided to have the chips removed. We returned to the store and waited through endless lines only to have a young technician hand us a pamphlet portraying two sad-looking teenagers. Yes, we could have the chips removed, but removal came with disastrous side effects: anxiety, social isolation, depression, suicide. We were reminded about our service contracts—the ones we'd signed but had never actually read. "Are you kidding?" we asked when the young salesperson showed us the contract. Would we really be paying this off for the next five years? Yes, the boy said. Even if the chip was removed? Yes, he said. What if we canceled our plan? We'd still be paying it off, he told us again, smiling gently.

We searched online and found blogs by parents explaining the tedious process of creating Parental Blocks. All we had to do was sync our accounts by left blinking and scrolling right with our eyes. We stopped reading and typed "parental blocks for parents without implants." We searched, we Googled, we navigated dead hyperlinks, we called toll-free numbers and sat on hold for hours simply to ask about setting up a password to our children's accounts. And at long last, a few of us succeeded in placing blocks on our children's usage.

Our children found ways around them easily.

We became vigilant. We canceled the connection to our apartments, opened our fuse boxes, shut off the electricity, and sat in candlelight with our furious children. They yelled at us, but we informed them we weren't going to relent. This was for their own good. We were their parents, we said, and we stood strong against them. It was only then, when we'd mounted our counteroffensive and held our ground, that our children retaliated.

How they gained access to our passwords, we have no clue. But here was a list of our past search histories and the emails we'd sent wherein we complained about bosses, or neighbors, or parents, or friends. Here were the porn sites we'd visited, the sexts sent to our partners. Here were databases upon databases of our most shameful secrets, tallied and collated. Our children stood in our living room. Did we understand how easy it would be for them to share this info with the world? they asked. They could make our private lives public with nothing more than wi-fi and a single blink of an eye.

"You can't do this," we told them.

"Of course we can," they said, looking at us as if we were toddlers.

"*Please*," we said, "don't do this."

And they smiled.

PURPLE HEART

When he thanks us for our service, the General raises his arms like a referee marking a touchdown, and the kids go wild. The adults join in too, hooting and hollering from the bleachers, and I wonder what I'm doing here, mashed into Baker Convention Center next to a guy in military fatigues and a "Make America Great Again" cap who's manspreading into my space. I look to my son, hoping he'll turn toward me and smile, but those days are gone; he just claps as the line of teenagers, adults, and a few middle-schoolers crosses the stage to have Valor Medals pinned to their fatigues.

"And now welcome our new Cadets!" the General announces. The parents in the front rows bring their preschoolers to the stage, lining them up to have Future

Courage medallions pinned to their chests, and I feel sick. I've told my son this whole event is one huge marketing scam—the medals are from China, the General just a costumed representative from VirtuCube who's recruiting online soldiers—but Eli doesn't care; he loves the games which promise him a social life.

High school wasn't an easy transition for Eli. He's small for his age and not good at sports; his only real interests are comics and video games. Whenever I picked him up from school, he was always standing alone by the curb, far from the groups of older boys whose conversations were peppered with war terminology.

After I saw that, I called my ex and asked whether we ought to reconsider Purple Heart. "He's being left out at school," I told her.

"Okay, that sucks, but the game is completely fucked. I'm not letting Eli kill real people in other countries."

"Apparently there's a non-combat mode. No droids, just avatars and simulation."

"No," she said, and I thought that was the end of it, but Eli must've overheard me. He worked on Colleen's family for the next three months, and that Christmas her parents bought the game for him. Colleen took it away immediately, but it was like returning a puppy on Christmas morning.

"I fucking hate the game," she finally said, "but if he's going to play, it'll be at your house."

So we agreed I'd take him to the upcoming convention, and afterward he could have Purple Heart as long as he played non-combat mode only.

And that's how our son's military training began.

※

"Non-combat," I tell Eli when we drive home from the convention.

"What about duty calls, skins, and hacker drones?" he asks.

"Are they available in non-combat?"

"No, but the game sucks without them. Next call starts Friday. I need to get enough valor points to even compete for a droid."

"You're not playing Combat Mode and you're not controlling droids. *Ever*. Do you understand?"

"Dad, avatars suck, they're just like stupid CGI with no real-world interface. The whole point is to see who gets picked for droid operation. Seriously, there were like literally over five hundred thousand civilian casualties in the last war. Guess how many since Purple Heart?" He looks at me, ready to parrot the statistics from their website.

"I don't care."

"One hundred and eight."

"You're fourteen years old. *I'm not letting you kill people.* Non-combat or you don't get to play."

"That sucks," Eli says, but he agrees. I give him the download code when we get home and he logs on.

There's a whole bunch of customization of the soldier's gender, race, and weaponry, and finally the game opens in a first-person shooter with a caravan of fifteen other avatars, their usernames listed along the periphery: cuddlybear125, jkillaz, infestation_g02, and my own son, FunkyMan15.

"Hostile forces have taken over the city," a Sergeant yells as the truck bumps along the streets. "We'll be entering the outskirts of Ankara. Your job: clean this mess up!"

"Sir, yes, sir!" my son says into his headphones.

"Soldiers, keep yourselves safe. The player with the most kills earns 5K valor points!"

"Sir, yes, sir!" my son yells from the safety of our living room. There's the squeal of the truck's brakes and a loud groan as the hatch opens, letting in the white glare of daylight. Then my son rises with the other soldiers and runs toward the staccato of gunfire.

There's no time to prepare for war. One moment I'm sitting with my son, wondering how long before action begins, and the next, he's in the midst of a simulated firefight on the streets of Ankara. A jeep carrying four masked insurgents screeches to a halt in front of us. There's the whiz of bullets and shattering glass, and then our screen is splattered with blood and my son's heartbeat thumps through the speakers. *You've been hit,* a female voice says. Eli unclips a grenade and tosses it, the explosion knocking him to the ground. When he rises, the jeep is burning and three of the men are on fire. Eli lowers the reticle onto a wounded terrorist's face and keeps the button pushed until the man's head blossoms into red spray. The screen splatters with more blood. *You've been hit,* the woman says again.

"Who's shooting you?" I yell.

"I don't know!"

You've been hit, the woman's voice repeats.

My son swivels. In the protective archway of a nearby building, a terrorist squeezes off a short burst, and my son's avatar jerks violently.

"Throw another grenade!"

"I can't, my arm's useless!"

Then it's all over. From the aerial view, we watch as the terrorist blasts my son's avatar apart, his body shaking from the shots.

A pop-up menu appears. *Thank you for your service. Want to fight again?*

"Whoa, that's a hard game," Eli says. He takes off his headset and extends the controller to me. "Want to try?"

I figure I'll have time to practice, but when I take the controls, a message pops onto the screen. *New convoy launching in 20 seconds. Join?*

"Say yes," Eli says, so I push the Start button but it just brings up the home screen with options to watch Netflix.

"Dad, press X2."

12 seconds to launch.

"Which one's X2?"

Nine seconds.

"The purple square on the side."

Six.

"Which side?"

"Dad! Left side!"

Four.

I find the button and press it, and suddenly Funky-Man15 is back in the carrier, the convoy gate open, the other players running down the ramp into the blinding sun as the sergeant yells for us to bring home the glory.

My avatar just sits on the bench blinking.

"Dad, what are you doing?"

"How do I get up?"

"Press A."

I tap the button and try to navigate the dual controls, but instead of rushing into battle, my avatar sprints toward the back of the truck and collides with the carrier's wall. *Be careful,* the female voice says. I get back onto my feet and gaze at the ceiling like an idiot.

"Dad, you suck."

I take a deep breath, focus on the controller, and turn my avatar toward the light. "Now what?"

"Press B3 to run."

I press the wrong button. My avatar takes out a grenade and pulls the pin.

"Dad! Throw it!"

"How do I throw?"

"Y! Y!"

"Where's the freaking Y button?"

"Blue square!"

My soldier throws the grenade out of the open carrier, completely reckless with no target in sight. It lands on the hood of a parked car and I watch as the other avatars flee. The car explodes, the impact sending me backward against the carrier wall.

Civilians are scattering and other avatars crouch in doorways as I navigate my soldier into the chaos I've caused. From a rooftop, a terrorist points an AK at me. There's a splatter of blood against the screen. *You've been hit.*

"Shoot him!"

I press the button for my machine gun, but my reticle scrolls wildly across the screen, blasting apart all the melons on a fruit seller's stand. *You've been hit.* My avatar's labored breath gasps through my headphones along with the pounding pulse of a simulated heartbeat. *You've been hit.* I tap the octagon button frantically, but my avatar just jumps in place with stupid little hops before the terrorist blasts me apart.

Thank you for your service. Want to fight again?

Eli takes back the controller. "Wow, Dad, you *really* suck."

"I hate that game," I say, and get up to make us mac and cheese.

By his fifth respawn, Eli's learned how to operate small ordnance, upgrade weapons, and use enhanced inter-rogation techniques. I watch him running around the computer-generated streets of Ankara, taking down insurgents who are nothing more than black dots on distant patios. He teams up with a group of high schoolers who are playing in Oslo and New Orleans, and they become a tight, efficient killing team, mowing down whole terrorist encampments and freeing a dozen Dutch hostages. I watch from the couch, no longer allowed to take a turn with his avatar, who's accumulated too many valor points to be sacrificed to my shitty gaming.

Outside, the snow is falling, the first storm of the season. Last year, a day like this would've led me to pull out the sled from the basement. We'd get suited up and make our way to the hill in town, take turns sledding, and return home red-cheeked for cocoa. Now the sun's already setting, the snow in our backyard blue with evening. We've been at war for over six hours.

"Okay," I say, rising from the couch. "Enough gaming, it's time to do homework."

"After this battle. You can't abandon your squad mid-game."

"How long until the battle's done?"

"I don't know. Maybe five minutes. Maybe an hour."

"*What?*"

But before he can explain, a sniper he hasn't seen takes him out. "Damn it," he says into his headset. "Hey guys, gotta go. Regroup tomorrow afternoon?"

"Yup."

"Totally."

And just like that, my son has friends.

I drop Eli off at his mom's on Sunday. No more simulated killing for another week. Back at the house, his socks are balled up on the couch, his dirty T-shirt on the floor along with half a dozen comics spread like playing cards across the carpeting. I gather his dirty laundry and bring his comic books to his room. He's still got his Spiderman poster on the wall and a dusty deck of Pokémon cards on his shelf, artifacts from a childhood that feels long gone now that he's started his war game. I return to grab the rest of his dirty clothes from the living room.

The system is blinking blue, waiting for another war to begin. I didn't always suck at video games. Back in the day I was a master of Grand Theft Auto and Fortnite. I could at least practice my gaming skills so I'm decent for the next time Eli comes to stay. And within minutes I'm logging on and crafting my own avatar and then I'm back in the trailer filled with soldiers.

"We've got two operative cells in this town," the Sergeant says. "Find them and take them out."

"Sir, yes, sir!" I say into the headset.

Glaring sunlight streams through the cargo doors and I breathe slowly, press the A button to rise, and navigate toward the street with my machine gun low and ready. There's no action, just cars driving by and a café where men are drinking coffee. I press the triangle button and my avatar lifts his gun toward the men.

"Easy there, buddy."

BlackHawk1372 is next to me, his light machine gun slung against his back. He takes out a pack of cigarettes, lights one, and extends the pack.

"Thanks," I say, though I have no clue how to take the cigarette. When I try to sling my gun, my avatar just uses it to jab the air.

"Okay, Tiger," BlackHawk says, "how about pressing your circle button twice to reholster. Octagon and L3 to pick up offered items. Inhale and exhale through your mic to puff." I follow his instructions, feeling like a teenager smoking for the first time. "Take it you're new to the game?"

"Pretty obvious, huh? It's my son's game," I say, before realizing I might be talking to someone younger than Eli. "Wait, how old are you?"

"Forty-six. Best advice: Take it slow. Biggest mistakes are made when you're panicking or trigger-happy. Check out that asshole." SemperFi4976 is by the café. He pulls a man off his chair and puts his boot on his head, then presses the barrel of his gun to the old man's temple. "I fucking hate that player. I've been on two missions with him so far. Doesn't care about gaining points, just wants to slaughter civilians every time. Come on, let's get out of here."

BlackHawk leads me down a side street where two

kids are playing ball against the side of a bakery. "Where are you playing from?" I ask.

"Santa Cruz," BlackHawk says, and flicks his cigarette. I can't figure out how to flick mine which is getting dangerously close to my avatar's fingers. "Triangle and R3 to put things down. Shit, you *really* don't know how to play, do you?"

"I skipped the tutorial," I admit, and locate the two buttons. My avatar flicks the cigarette to the ground. "Where's all the action?"

"Sometimes you get towns like this. There's one or two terrorists hiding in this whole place, but really it's a sniper playground. You get assholes like SemperFi back there sacrificing valor points to watch civilians explode. I'd take him out if they let me, but we can't shoot our own. Go ahead and try."

"What?"

"Take your handgun by pressing G, point it at my head, pull the trigger."

"I'm not about to do that."

"Fucking try it already, you'll see what I mean."

So I unholster my gun and point it at BlackHawk. The kids have stopped playing ball and are watching us. "Now what?"

"Press the triangle."

I push the button but nothing happens. I press it again. My avatar won't even move his finger. On the screen a red message flashes: *Invalid Target*.

"Like I said, I'd blow that guy's head off, but they don't let you. I'm Brogan." He reaches out for a shake.

"Paul," I say, but my avatar just stands there looking at Brogan's extended hand.

"Triangle and L3," Brogan instructs, and my avatar reholsters his gun and shakes his hand. "Tell you what, this mission's bullshit, let's get a car and I'll take you outside the city. We can detonate some C4, handle Claymores, practice some basic gameplay."

We find a car idling outside a gas station and Brogan yanks the driver out, then drives us to a field far from town where he teaches me how to roll and shoot, detonate C4, and drive while lobbing grenades out the window. He hands me a cigarette when we take a break from blowing things up, and this time I light it easily. "You said this is your son's game?"

"Yeah, he'd flip if he knew I was playing. His mom and I didn't let him play for over a year."

"Married?"

"Divorced. Three years ago."

"Shit, sorry to hear it. If you're interested, there's a place around here I can take you. Girl players who'll fuck avatars."

"Are you serious?"

"Not my thing—but if you'd be into it . . ."

"I'm good."

"All right, man. Well, wife's calling, gotta log off."

"Jeez, it's three a.m. Sorry, I had no clue how late it was."

"No worries. Still midnight here. I'm back tomorrow at eight p.m., West Coast time. Just request a mission with me and we'll find something better than this sniper bull-shit. I'm actually a higher-level player, but once you get to the upper ranks it's a whole lot of teens and psychos."

"Sounds good."

"Cool," Brogan says. "See you tomorrow."

And just like that, I have a new friend.

I have to admit that war, despite its terror, is a bonding experience. When Eli comes over on the weekends we talk about strategies, discuss levels, and go to conventions together. We're in the bleachers on Valentine's Day when the General welcomes Sergeant Franks, the keynote speaker, a sixty-five-year-old, real-war, Purple Heart vet-eran from the Desert Storm days. Franks is clean-shaven and when he leans toward the microphone his voice is steady and cold.

"I'm Sergeant Franks of the First Infantry Regiment, Second Battalion, Third Brigade. I did two tours in Iraq. Went over in 1990 to take out Saddam, didn't do it the first time, so went back and got the job done. Lost my limb in armed combat." He gestures to his pinned-up sleeve. "That's a joke. You can laugh." No one does. He reaches over and tugs at the pinned cuff, and for a moment I worry he's going to show us the amputation, but he just lets go and leans back into the microphone. "You're all doing very courageous work protecting this country and eliminating our enemy without ever having to get hurt. Thanks to Purple Heart, you don't have to think about VA hospitals, or nights when you can't sleep because you're aching so bad it makes you scream." The rustling of potato chip bags has stopped; even the kids down front aren't moving. "So, I just want to let you know that this soldier, who served on the ground, congratulates you for playing a game. And, on behalf of Purple Heart, I say thank you for your service."

The General takes the microphone from Franks. "Let's stand and give a proud salute to Sergeant Franks!" We all rise and put our hands to our foreheads as a uni-formed girl in military cutoffs leads him to the side of the stage, where he awards Medals of Honor to the top five gamers, a mix of high schoolers and middle-aged men like me.

After the ceremony, there's a frenzy to buy games, posters, and pins. The late-winter sunshine lights the lobby in a soft glow, which would be peaceful if it weren't for the chaos of a thousand kids and adults crowding merch tables. It's not as horrible a scene as I used to think it was. Mostly just men talking with each other about the game, a bunch of young women in Sergeant Nightingale costumes hawking stickers, and all our kids excited about the junk they've bought.

Eli wants to stay until the end, says they'll hook us up with free gear once they close, but it's a rumor that turns out not to be true. The sellers just pack up their supplies and wheel them out, and the hall is empty by the time we leave, the parking lot vacant except for a handful of scattered pickups and a single station wagon parked by ours.

"Isn't that the sergeant?" Eli asks.

Sure enough, Sergeant Franks is leaning against his station wagon as we approach our car. "You proud to serve your country?" he asks Eli.

"Yes, sir," my son says.

"What's your name, soldier?"

"Eli."

"How long you been playing?"

"A couple months, but I'm not controlling droids yet," Eli says and looks at me.

"Well, that's not a horrible thing," Sergeant Franks says. "I think your dad's probably just looking out for you. At least you won't be killing anyone."

Eli nods. "Yeah, but I'd be a great soldier. I'd go in there and take down insurgents, dodge and roll, set off some C-4."

Sergeant Franks is listening to Eli, but he's grimacing like everything my son is saying hurts. When Eli starts in about hijacking tanks, Franks cuts him off.

"That's not what war's like," he says, his voice grim. "It's not something you can spend fifty bucks on and turn off when you're done. Wish I could, but I can't. I'll tell you something: Not everyone you end up killing deserves to die. You understand? *You understand?*" he barks at my son.

"Come on," I say, and put my arm around Eli. I click the fob and our car beeps open.

"Damn, I'm sorry," Sergeant Franks says. His face goes slack, the anger gone as quickly as it appeared. "Seriously, I'm really sorry. I didn't mean to get angry." Franks takes a soft pack of cigarettes from his breast pocket, shakes one loose into his mouth, and lights it. "Look, they'd fire me if they heard me say this, but it's not actually fun to kill people. I've seen real death. I had a lot of buddies who died. They're training you to kill without remorse." He lets out a cloud of smoke, looking just like my avatar when I smoke with Brogan. "Hey, I've got something for you, okay?" Franks opens the rear latch and roots around the back of his car until he locates a cigar box. "Here, soldier. Want one of these?" Inside the box are dozens of shining Medals of Honor.

"Whoa," Eli says.

"Go ahead, take one," Franks says. "I'm not supposed to give them away, but they give me hundreds. Funny, all I wanted was a medal like this." He rattles the box, and Eli takes one. Sergeant Franks taps his chest with the box where his Purple Heart hangs. "Instead I got this one."

"Thank you for the medal," I say, taking out my wallet, "and thank you for your service." I pull a twenty and extend it, but Franks just stands there looking at me as though I'm trying to hand him a dirty sock.

"I don't want your money," he says, his voice loud in the empty lot. "All I want is for the kid to understand what he's headed for."

⚡

Sergeant Franks spooked something in Eli, because after we get home he doesn't want to play Purple Heart. I ask him what's wrong, but he just says he'd rather watch funny videos on YouTube. Later, he comes out to where I'm sitting.

"Want to go biking?" he asks.

So we bicycle to the library, where we look at the old DVDs in the dwindling media section and find a comedy to watch. Later that night we make nachos and watch the movie, and it's cozy not to be fighting terrorists for a change. When I say good night to Eli, I ask him if anything's wrong.

"It just kinda sucks not to get to play Combat Mode," he says. "Besides, now that I have a Medal of Honor, there's like no point anymore."

"So you're done with the game?"

"I don't know. That guy made me feel bad about wanting to play Combat."

"Well, it's like he said, right? It's probably a good thing not to kill people."

"I guess," Eli says.

After he's asleep, I spend the next three hours gaming with Brogan. My ex would be appalled if she could see me, a forty-three-year-old man drinking beer and playing video games like an adolescent, but it's fun. My gaming skills have improved, and over the last month my avatar's gained higher ranks as we bomb and destroy villages. I'm on my third IPA and playing with a buzz when we liberate a whole compound of American journalists.

My screen turns golden. *Congrats, you're one of our top players! Ready for Combat Mode?*

"Shit," I say to Brogan. "I just unlocked Combat Mode."

"That's fucking awesome. Accept it!"

"I'm not sure I'm ready for that."

"Why not? I'm already combat approved. We'll try our first real mission together. We're a great team. We haven't killed a single civilian—shit, we're saving people. Let's fucking do this."

Blasting through my headphones, the US Army Band plays the celebratory strains of "Architect of Victory," my heart pounding to its beat. I click Yes and the screen fills with scrolling boilerplate language that concludes with the question *Accept Military Enlistment?* I click Yes again, and then we're back in a carrier, the screen no longer animated but a live feed streaming from a GoPro camera attached to a droid's head.

"Jesus," I say.

"Yep, this is for real," Brogan says. "Don't worry, I've got your back. You ready?"

"Sure," I manage to say before the carrier comes to a halt. Then Brogan and I are out in the actual streets of Ankara. We follow coordinates, dodge snipers, kick down the doors of a local mosque, and vaporize a terrorist. Just as we're finishing him off, an American soldier emerges in the mosque's doorway and aims at us.

"Why's he aiming at—" My droid's body jerks from

the sudden impact of bullets, and my camera lens shatters into a spiderwebbed feed of the mosque's domed ceiling. I turn back toward the American droid, lower my gun and try to pull the trigger. *Invalid Target.*

"What the fuck?" I yell, searching for cover, but there's nowhere to hide. The American takes aim again and destroys us both. My screen turns black.

Thank you for your service. Ready to fight again?

"Damn," Brogan says. "We were solid until the Ambot showed up. Sorry, should've warned you, resistance hacked some of our droids. They can shoot us, but we can't take them down."

"How do you defeat them?"

"Only hope is to locate their gamers, but they're holed up in secret cells throughout the city with other hacked droids protecting them. It's basically a suicide mission. You need top-level valor to even try it. Well, that ended badly, but welcome to your first mission."

"Thanks," I say, my heart still pounding.

"Okay, wife's calling. Tomorrow same time? Brush up on your skills and maybe we'll get access to go after those gamer cells one day."

"Definitely," I say, and though Brogan logs off, I decide to try my hand at war one more time.

I don't tell Eli I'm playing Combat Mode, but I show him my skills in non-combat and ask him for pointers, and after he's gone to bed, I log on to war with Brogan, gain valor points, and help free hostages across the ocean. It's deep into spring, the last icy rains splattering the living room windows, when Brogan and I unlock Gamer Cell Mode.

"You ready to try this?" Brogan asks.

"Totally."

We accept the mission, and find ourselves in a smaller van with four other top-level gamers, heading toward an apartment complex where a terrorist cell is operating hacked droids. The coordinates of the gamers hover along the periphery, their red dots flashing on our maps.

"Am-bots are protecting the gamers," our Sergeant says. "I'm not going to lie, probably none of you are going to make it out of this. But even if you get blasted, as long as you take those gamers down, you've accomplished your mission and will earn ten thousand valor points. You understand."

"Sir, yes, sir."

The van opens, and there, between the four apartment buildings, are a half dozen Am-bots patrolling the area.

"Follow me!" I yell to Brogan, and for the first time I'm leading the mission, running my son's game plan with smoke grenades as cover to keep us moving forward. The sound of gunfire echoes off the buildings, and behind us, DesertWolf08 goes down, followed by Jerzyboy18. Brogan throws another smoke grenade to shield our way through the front door of the apartment building.

"Am-bots still on us!" he yells as we take the staircase. Down below there's the sound of boots and a rattle of gunfire. We crash into the second-floor hallway, forty feet from the gamer cell and closing. Behind us, the stairwell door smashes open. I position myself solidly in front of the apartment at the end of the hall and kick it open to reveal the pale light of a flat-screen. Two hackers are on the couch controlling the Am-bots. I raise my machine gun and let off a burst of bullets that catches them as they turn. The red dots of our targets disappear from our map.

Congratulations! You've just eliminated two leaders of the insurgency.

"Search the bodies," Brogan orders as he secures the door.

The room is hard to navigate in the darkness. There's only the blue light of the television illuminating the bodies. On the screen, the Am-bots they were controlling stand motionless, and for a moment the double vision of seeing the game within the game on my own screen is disorienting. I keep expecting my controller to move the small figures on the apartment's flat-screen, so I focus on the ground instead, my GoPro projecting the mess of the room. There are food containers on the floor, empty plastic bottles, and dirty clothes. There's a blast of gunfire outside.

"Hurry up!" Brogan yells.

I round the couch, the light of the screen flickering against the gamers' bodies. It's when I see their faces that my weapon slumps toward the ground.

The boys on the couch are no older than Eli. Between them is an empty tube of Pringles and an open carton of Ikram biscuits. One of the boys had been holding a plastic bottle of Fanta, which is now in his lap, the orange soda spilling onto him and the floor in a fizzing, widening circle.

"They're kids," I say.

"They're not kids, they're insurgents. Come on, we got Am-bots to deal with! Stay with me now, don't log off!"

I log off.

The house is quiet. My half-finished beer is on the coffee table, my abandoned controller in my lap, the system blinking blue. Beside me is an opened bag of corn chips, which I stare and stare at. I'm not sure how long I sit there, frozen. All I know is that when I finally rise, I cross the room to the console, hold down the power button, and wait for the blue light to die.

It's late spring now, long past the final snow. Michigan is warming up. Soon school will let out. Weekends, Eli goes to play with his new friends, who have parents more lenient than me. Good people who just want their kids to have playdates again. He drinks juice boxes and eats Cheetos and fights the latest war. Then he bicycles home for dinner and I pretend everything's normal—that he's simply a kid coming home from a playdate, where they did nothing more horrible than play video games and drink too much soda—hoping he's telling me the truth when he says they aren't playing Combat Mode.

Eli's anger at me lasted for almost a month after he'd

found out I'd played Combat. I explained to him that I'd
made a mistake, that I'd killed people, that the game was
evil. "It's not evil, you're just a sloppy gamer," Eli said,
and I lost it on him. Some small part of me watched as I
yelled, aware that it wasn't an enemy I was destroying but
my relationship with my son.

At night I lie awake. I think about Brogan back at the
beginning of the game, trolling users for a new buddy. I
think about Sergeant Franks in the parking lot, warning
me about what awaits after you're done killing. Mostly
though, I think about that moment before I pulled the
trigger. In my mind, I rewrite history. I ease off the triangle button, lower my weapon, log off forever. The boys
live.

Some nights there's no sleep, and my son finds me at
the breakfast table, red-eyed and hollow. He lets me hug
him good morning, seems to understand that I need it
more than him, that somehow his father isn't the same
person anymore. "It's just a stupid game," he says as he
hugs me, and I put my arms around him, hold him close
for as long as I can before he tells me it's enough, that it's
time to let him go.

TRUE LOVE TESTIMONIALS

CLÖE

Empty? I wouldn't say it's empty. I guess there're guys on make-an-av sites creating shells to have sex with, and that's kinda empty. They're afraid to even *text* girls in real life; like they actually freeze up anytime a woman talks to them because they're only used to hump-avs. Which is pretty sad. But, in general, it's like life. You can have empty sex or meaningful sex. It's kinda based on who you're hooking up with and why you're there.

I guess if you're looking for suggestions, it'd be nice if you had an option where you could log off but still let your av stay on. Because I feel bad for dudes sometimes. Like, I know guys say the bodysuit cuts down on feeling— and when I first heard that, I was like, Um, please don't fix that—but sometimes they can't stay hard and then they need all this reassurance, or even if they stay hard it just takes too long. Then you have to stop before they get off, or you don't say anything and just endure it. It's definitely not ideal.

So, if I had the option, I'd totally get out of my body-suit while the dude got himself off with my av. Like, if my av could be with him and it could say encouraging things automatically? Like a text-to-talk option, so I could be in bed and feed my av dialogue? That'd be way more compassionate than ghosting mid-sex once I've come—which, whatever, tons of dudes don't think twice about ghosting once they're done, but some guys are sweet. So, no, I don't think it's empty. I just wish you'd add an option so I could go to sleep and my av would finish him off, and kiss him, and say goodnight, and even lie with him for a while. That way we could both hold each other, and he'd never even know I wasn't there.

BRETT

I was reading about the number of guys who present as girls—so, that's like a pretty common thing, right? You probably have percentages on that? Really? So what are they? Fuck, that's a lot.

Whatever, no judgment, it's just that if I want to be with a woman, I want to know it's a woman. And, yeah, sometimes I present as a girl—but that's usually because I know the guy is actually a girl presenting as a guy. It's not like I want actual guys to fuck me. I'm just saying that sometimes being fucked instead of doing the fucking is a pretty cool part about the whole thing, right? That's kinda your whole ad campaign.

But like, if usernames don't mean shit, and you don't offer gender verification like ChristianSwing, then of course you're going to have my kind of complaints. Because I was with this really beautiful Latina user who was, like, straight out of porn, super thick lips, sexy voice, and we had *incredible* sex. And afterwards, we're lying there and talking in one of my favorite spaces. It's a mash-up of my past actual rooms, like my high school bedroom and my dorm room, and then my fantasized living space, so it's pretty personal to me. There's a whole wall that's a lava lamp with purple and blue jelly, and it was lighting up the bed where we were lying, watching the blobs stretching and floating, and Jenna says, "Can I tell you something?" I say sure, because I figure she's about to tell me she likes me—and she does, she says she feels a really deep connection with me. But then she says, "So . . . my name's actually Ron." And I'm like, *"What?"* "Yeah," Ron says. "I'm using in Taos, New Mexico. Sorry I didn't tell you before we made love." And meanwhile Ron's saying all this in Jenna's voice with her beautiful lips and that sexy lisp she makes with her tongue—and it just fucked me up. Because I was a hundred percent sure there was no way she was a guy. "Listen," Jenna's saying, "I really like what we have here together—" And that's when I blocked Ron completely. Like, see you, dude, you're fucking blacklisted.

So that fucked me up for a while. And, I get it, verifying's up to us, but for real, your whole *Try meeting in a neutral CoffeeShop*—nobody's ever doing that. The most anyone asks is "So, you're a girl, right?" "Yeah, and you're a dude, right?" And, okay, maybe that's not very responsible, but nobody's trying to be Sherlock Holmes. And the thing is, I just keep thinking about Jenna. Like, if Ron presents as Jenna, but she's hot and nice, what's wrong with seeing her again? Even if I knowingly know? It's a female avatar, right? So, like, it's still cool to call myself straight, right? Like, what do *you* think?

7

I don't use it for sex. Been there, done that. I was one of your first subscribers. Besides, I host morphing orgies. I don't know how much you know about that scene, but it's a very social scene. Very sexual. Lots of entities trying out eros-fluid bodies, lots of partying, lots of drugs. Honestly, it's a little too much.

So for the past year, when I need a break, I've been using your site as a space to be alone. I crafted an apartment that looks like a New York loft. It has an enormous window that overlooks the Brooklyn Bridge, and I'll go there and sit on the couch just looking out my window at the city, imagining everyone out there having all that sex. I might mix myself a drink, or even watch a film. I realize it's crazy to spend that kind of money just to watch a film in my bodysuit, but I have the money, and I like the *meta* of it. I'll just sit there for a couple hours, relax, play a game of solitaire, or Sudoku. Sometimes I'll just sing. That's right, sing. *I know.* A lot of monthly fees and wasted matchmaking potential, but that's what I enjoy doing. Write that down as my kink if you want: I sing.

SHELLY

Maybe two times a week? Three at most? I take av breaks though, go celibate, because it can get pretty depressing. Last night during the dinner rush I actually heard a guy say, "Why would I *want* to date real women?" Which is just really, really . . . ugh . . . it pisses me off. Like, okay, so now that you can fuck whatever girl you want, you're just going to craft some super-impossible-body-size avatar of your adolescent dreams and go jerk off into her because real women are expendable? Except when you want kids, right? Which is probably next. You guys are probably already developing that? No fucking way. Great, so soon people like that guy will just have children online because it'll be much easier for dudes like him not to have to deal with toilet training. No late nights or early mornings, no Mom, just some little clone of himself who he'll call Junior and upload whenever he feels lonely about not having a real wife, or real kids, or a real house instead of a tiny empty efficiency where he's in his bodysuit 24/7.

So yeah, thanks, the dating scene in the real world sucks. All the actual dudes my age are online, so who am I supposed to date? A bunch of bearded, gray-haired millennials all trying to be retro and calling any dinner date they take me on *vintage*. For real? This past New Year's Eve—*New Year's fucking Eve*—I worked a double with this cute busser that seemed really cool, superintelligent and funny. He was studying immersive design and knew all these avant-garde atmosphere artists. We were having a smoke break out back and it started snowing, big flakes landing on the dumpster and the cars, and it was really beautiful. I was brushing the flakes out of his hair and flirting with him. We'd snuck out a bottle of champagne and were trading swigs, and it felt really good. Like how my parents described what it was like back in the day when they fell in love. And so I said, Fuck it, and I put my hand behind his head and kissed him. And he *literally* didn't know what to do. He just kept flicking his tongue from side to side over my lips like he was trying to activate my mouth sensor, and I was, like, No. Fucking. Way. Then he pulls away and says, "We should meet online after work." And I'm like, Yeah, that'd be cool, but I have to get up early to virtual-sit my friend's puppy. But, whatever, I was feeling lonely, so I logged on that night after I got home and we had sex, because I didn't want to be by myself for the start of the New Year.

So, yeah, I guess two times a week, maybe three. Sometimes more.

JEROME

Call me old-fashioned, but I enjoy them. Are they a waste of money? Maybe. But do you watch 9D films? Listen to audio-immersive novels? And just because you're not actually *in* that film or book, are those a waste of money? Isn't all pleasure constructed through immaterial worlds and virtual bodies just a form of aesthetic preference? And maybe this is the Buddhist in me speaking—but what are any of these sensory delights if not our own projections of desire in drag? Better yet, I have a friend who collects books. You probably think that's an antiquated hobby, but that's what gives him pleasure. He doesn't read them, just loves their smell, their feel, how they look lined up on his shelves. That's his delight.

So my pleasure is Restaurants. And I find men of my age enjoy them as well. Yes, eating is strange. Yes, you're essentially just sitting there in your bodysuit kissing the air over and over. And yes, if you want my feedback, develop that technology, improve it, offer better hardware. The best I've found so far is from GastroSense, a silicone mouth guard that lets you actually spoon real food into your mouth and chew, or sort of chew. I'll cook myself something at home, then put on the bodysuit and mouth guard, and sit and eat. Oh, I don't know, potatoes or noodles, I'll chop up some papaya, just something soft to chew while I'm having seared duck with my date and talking like people once did. Honestly, I've been out with some guys just for dinner, nothing more. I'm talking three-hour dinners. It's better than sex. Sweetheart, av-guys are a dime a dozen. I can get sex every night if I wanted until the bodysuit rubs me raw. But you find those rare men who actually want to sit with you and have a conversation, or simply hold your hand as you share something from your past—that's worth every dollar I spend my retirement on.

BRANDON

Fuck yeah, I overlay faces. Plenty of guys do that. I'll flick through them while we're fucking. For real, bro [laughs]. I know, that's super fucked up, right? Do you think that's fucked up? It's kinda fucked up, right? [laughs]. But, whatever, if it was *that* fucked up then why do you make it an option? Besides, girls don't know. They're probably doing the same thing. Serious, it's like, sometimes you just been going at it for too long and you need a change-up to help you over the edge. Like, okay, I'm done with the brunette right now, maybe a blonde can help, or like an Asian, or some girl with extra-blue eyes. I've got like a dozen favorite faces in rotation, and I'll just swipe through them to help me out. Is that fucked up? It's kinda fucked up, right? [laughs].

SABLE

Just once. It was actually my ex-husband—who looked nothing like himself. My ex is a fifty-year-old pasty-white stock trader who's about five-four; Alberto was thirty-eight, chiseled, and Italian. It wasn't until we were having sex that I recognized him. It's incredible how you can still know someone just from the way they hold you. So

I asked: *"Jonathan?"* Until I asked aloud, I was worried he'd hacked my account. Do you even have a policy about that? You do? Oh, yeah, well, who reads any of that, right?

So I said his real name, and Alberto, or Jonathan, sort of jumped back on the bed. I mean, here's this previously uber-confident Latin lover looking at me completely frightened and timid and covering himself with a pillow. I could see scared little Jonathan through his eyes. "How do you know my name?" he asks. And I say, "Jon, it's me, Elizabeth." And he jumps off the bed and covers up his body with the crumpled sheets, very freaked out, saying it's twisted *of me* to do something like this. And I'm just laughing. I couldn't help myself. I mean, this is the opposite of ideal, right? Here's Alberto looking all crease-browed, exactly like Jonathan used to look, and accusing me of av-stalking him. Well, *that* took a while to figure out. But, to Jonathan's credit, he didn't log off. He actually came back to the bed and sat down and told me I looked amazing. I don't know if I should've taken that as a compliment or an insult. I've spent a lot on upgrades and I'm proud of Sable—she looks like how I feel inside, even though . . . well . . . I *actually* look like a fifty-six-year-old mother of two college kids: overworked, stressed out, financially struggling, like someone who would benefit from online yoga. "You look great too, *Alberto,*" I said. Because I liked seeing my ex in Alberto's body. He'd been confident and dominant in a way I *really* liked. And though I wanted to tease him about it, I also thought: Okay, maybe this is who Jonathan always was inside. Like, perhaps all along the two of us have lived with these hidden avatars within us, and it was those other human profiles named Elizabeth and Jonathan who were the false personalities. Like maybe, if we could've been Alberto and Sable all along, we never would've gotten divorced.

We've started seeing one another again. We rendezvous about five or six times a week. Sometimes I'll just log on and lie in bed with him, tell him about my day, and he'll listen, which is something Jonathan never did. I'd say the past six months with Alberto have been the best months Jon and I ever spent together.

JENNIE & SUSAN

Yeah, we're *that* couple. We met through your site at one of those free, twenty-four-hour mingle-trials. It was a one-in-a-million chance. She lives in Eugene and I'm in Jersey, and I logged on figuring the whole place would be filled with straight guys pretending to be lesbians. Like, okay, you and you are total phonies, and you're using your wife's account right now. Plus, apparently, it was a coast-to-coast mingle; I didn't know how insane those are.

SUSAN [takes Jennie's hand]: *She's not techy at all.*

First of all, I don't like crowds. Second, I don't like immersive reality. And what do I choose: a nationwide event with that buffet table that stretches all the way into infinity. I mean, it's nice what you do, but it's a little Dalí to see that table going on forever with all these thirty-five- to fifty-year-old women mingling and eating virtual strawberries. I was thinking, *Yeah, this is going to last ten minutes.*

SUSAN: *She was there for an hour by the time we met.*

Worst hour of my life! I don't know how anyone can handle those mingles. I'm just passing by one woman after another, not getting pinged by anyone. I finally meet this woman who green-lines me and we talk for a second, but the moment she finds out I'm in landscaping, she becomes a ghost. So basically I'm in this room filled with more and more ghosts, window-shopping for women to green-line, and mostly plunking femmes I don't match with. I was actually starting to take a kind of sick pleasure in it—like it was a mafia game. Um, nope, not you. *Plunk.* Not you either. *Plunk.* I'm just taking woman after woman out, making them ghost-bodies. Seriously, I don't know how anyone can stand those mixers for a full twenty-four hours.

SUSAN: *But then you saw me.*

She was over by the buffet table, getting a strawberry, and we looked at each other and green-lined immediately. And I know I sound cheesy, but, yeah, our eyes met across a crowded room.

SUSAN: *I love when you sound cheesy.*

How long did we actually stay there?

SUSAN: *Six minutes.*

We exchanged user IDs and both of us were like, Um, it's a little crowded here. Want to sign up and rent a private space somewhere? She said, *The Tropics?* and I said,

You bet, and we both swiped Yes for membership and, well, you get the picture.

SUSAN: *That was the best first date I've ever been on. We've been together for seven years.*

Well, at least online.

SUSAN: *Hm. She has a husband in real life. Which I don't want to know about. I mean, online it's just the two of us and that's it.*

Really though, East–to–West Coast plane tickets? One ticket is enough for a year of service. And for what? So we can "see" each other for a weekend. Even if we could afford the trip, the hubby would never go for it.

SUSAN: *Maybe we don't get to hold hands, like real hands, but that's fine—it's not like we need to do that. Besides, like she said, real life isn't part of the agreement.*

She's happy, I'm happy. Yeah, we're essentially the poster girls for you guys. So, go ahead and quote us, you gave us True Love.

CHILDHOOD

They arrived in boxes on a rainy August morning, their ETA marked on their parents' calendar with the words *Joey & Lacy's Birthday*, and they emerged into the world at ten and fourteen, a memory they often talked about in their separate beds.

What did he remember?

Rumbling, Joey said. The room's darkness reminded him of the truck, though he wasn't sure if that was a real memory. Had that been real? What about the Grand Canyon? They'd ridden mules down to the base, set up tents, and spent the night by the Colorado River.

"Think about it, how old were you?" Lacy asked.

"Eight."

"You weren't even launched yet."

"What about the blizzard, then?" The cars had been

buried beneath the snow, and when their mother opened the back door, there was ice stacked higher than him.

"Never happened," Lacy said.

Joey marveled at the way memories became smaller once you realized they weren't real. Like perfectly contained snow globes, ready to be placed alongside the other globes of elementary school, sleepaway camp, and vacations their family would've taken had there been enough money.

Money was the reason their parents gave when presenting them with their beds in the shared room. The beds were neatly made, a stack of towels resting by their pillows, and on each a present: a dress for Lacy, a soccer ball for Joey, both with a small handmade card, the edges crooked from their mother's scissors. *Welcome to our family.*

This wasn't how it was done in real families, Lacy said. Boys and girls didn't share the same room. And their parents understood that, but they couldn't afford a bigger house. There were overdue statements for the children amassing on the dining room table, alongside electricity, heating, and mortgage bills. So Joey and Lacy shared the room, their beds on either side, and they spent their pre-dreaming hours trying to remember the past.

"Was the UP trip real?" Joey asked. They'd rented kayaks and paddled to Pictured Rocks. Dad had tipped over his kayak and splashed into Lake Superior, and his shoes had squished all day.

"Of course *that* happened. We have photos," Lacy said.

Above them, stars arced across the water-stained ceiling. Their mother had bought the night-light after they'd returned from the UP. It hadn't been Christmas or his birthday, just a sale in the toy aisle of Target where she'd let him wander. When she came to get him, he'd shown her the night-light and she'd looked at the price, then placed it in the cart for no other reason than to make him happy.

That, at least, was a real memory, filled entirely with love.

You weren't supposed to remove your emotion card. It wasn't a rule anyone had ever told Joey, just something he knew. Like how you shouldn't peel back your skin-reserve pouch—that was there for when your frame expanded—and you never took out your eyes, though your parents could shut you down to replace them, and when you went swimming, you always checked the back of your head to make sure the USB covering was in place. Joey had once placed the flat edge of his toothbrush against the small flesh-covered slit beneath his armpit, but it felt gross, like flipping your eyelids inside out or sticking your finger too deep in your belly button. And so, on the night of his upgrade, he sat dutifully on the closed toilet seat as his mother put on rubber gloves.

"It was a fun summer, wasn't it?" she asked. She used the rectangular tool to push his release tab while distracting him by talking about how he'd soon be in middle school. It was going to be exciting, she said, and he heard the pop of his emotion card releasing before everything grew colorless. Then there was no warmth left in the shell of his body, just a deep, metallic coldness, and the roughness of a strange woman's fingers fiddling with his armpit. She took a new card from its plastic casing and pressed the world back into him with a flush of warmth and color, her voice full of love again. "All done. You're eleven now—big, big stuff," she said, wiping the tears from his eyes.

When, later, Joey saw his sister remove her new card in the dim light of the constellation lamp, he reminded her she wasn't supposed to do that.

"There's a lot of things we're programmed not to do, Joey. I want to know what happens when you do them." Lacy put her emotion card on the bedside table and climbed beneath her sheets. "Besides, Mom and Dad aren't our parents. They're just consumers who've learned to be really nice to their robots."

Joey hated when she used that word. He knew they weren't human, but that didn't mean he didn't have emotions. Like the coziness he felt upon opening his lunchbox to discover a note his mom had packed for him, or how she'd bring him a juice box when she picked him up, or how his father played soccer with him in the backyard after work. All of it—the programmed memories and the real ones—was filled with love. Joey placed his hand against his pajamas, felt his heart beating beneath his palm, steady and comforting. Even if it was just a small machine-powered balloon inflating and deflating, it let out a pulse like a real heartbeat.

"Well, I feel like they're my parents," he said to the darkness.

Lacy turned on her side to face him, the whites of her eyes blue in the glow of the night-light. "That's because they program you to feel that way. They have percentages for the amount of emotions we get."

"How do you know?"

"I logged into their account. Know how much independent thought we have? Fifteen percent. Timmy and Issa have zero. That's why they're so weird. I read it in an email their parents sent Mom and Dad."

Joey used to play Legos with Timmy. Every time Timmy would hand him a plastic brick, he'd tell him he could put it on the spaceship. After the eighth piece, Timmy had seemed creepy. He'd extended the Lego toward Joey, smiling. *You're our guest. You can put the next piece on.*

"Know what Mom and Dad set our love at? One hundred percent."

"So?"

"So, that's messed up—we shouldn't have to be programmed to love them. But we're just complicated, expensive toys. Whatever, you're too young to get it." She turned her head away, the blue light of the room illuminating her cheekbones, and Joey could almost see the metal frame beneath her skin.

His tears had nothing to do with the sensitivity his parents had programmed for him. It was a personal feeling, and though he couldn't grasp its source, he felt the wetness on his cheeks as he stared at the constellations. Lacy sighed heavily and turned. *"What?"* He didn't answer, just lay there feeling tears rolling out of him, his heart aching. "Joey, come on," she said. Then, more softly, "What's wrong?"

Joey wiped the sleeve of his Spiderman pajamas against his face. "If Mom and Dad are consumers then how do you feel about me? Am I even your brother?"

What he needed was a single word uttered with her heart's resonance, even if it was just a balloon inflating and deflating. Instead, she took a deep breath. "You know you are," she said in the exact same tone she used when lying to their parents.

He was supposed to have soccer practice that Monday, but the coach went home with food poisoning, and his mother called the office to say she couldn't get out of work early. Timmy's mom would drive him; Lacy would be there by the time he got back.

The trees had begun to turn colors and the leaves fell around the car as they drove home. Timmy asked friendly questions about school. What was his favorite subject? Smile. Did he like his teachers? Smile. What was he going to be for Halloween? Smile. Want to go trick-or-treating together?

When Joey got home, music was blasting from upstairs.

He heard voices and coughing as he climbed the staircase toward the smell of burning plastic, and when he opened their bedroom door he found Lacy sitting on his bed by the cracked window. Her face was bright from the sunlight filtering through the trees outside, the whole room golden with the tint of the oak's leaves. Another boy was on his bed, crumpling Joey's Avengers blanket beneath his shoes. The boy had Lacy's emotion card in his hand and was using a metal file against it, scraping shavings thin as fluff into a folded piece of paper. Lacy held a lighter to a glass tube, and the pipe glowed molten yellow with a puff of black smoke.

"Fuck!" she said when she saw Joey. Her exhalation pierced the room, and she buried her face in his blankets, her body shaking so hard Joey thought she was choking until he saw her teeth grinning. The guy scraping the card grabbed a can of air freshener and sprayed it in a wide arc, the room suddenly synthetic with mango.

"Hey, lil guy," he said, sliding the scraped card into Lacy's armpit. "Cool room. You like the Avengers, huh?"

"What are you guys doing?" Joey said to his sister.

Lacy just continued to grin, and the kid with the air freshener folded the paper on the bed into a makeshift envelope, carefully securing the remaining filings, before tucking everything into his backpack. He put his hand on Lacy's back and shook her. "Hey, we should go. I can drive."

Lacy sat up crookedly, her mouth tight. "My fucking brother," she said and laughed so hard that a streak of spit glistened on her chin. "Don't tell Mom and Dad," she said as the boy helped her down the stairs, and they stumbled together to the front door.

From the upstairs bedroom, Joey watched them drive away. The leaves rustled from a warm breeze which blew through the cracked window, everything stinking of mango and burnt plastic. His Avengers blanket was a mess, and his mom would be home in an hour. So he picked up the air freshener and sprayed the room again before going downstairs to find the fan his dad kept stored in the basement.

When Lacy came home that night, her eyes weren't red anymore, but the sides of her mouth still curled upward in a grin, and it was only later, when they were in bed, that her smile disappeared. She lay on her side, watching Joey. "Thanks for not telling Mom and Dad," she said. "You're a cool little brother."

"Why were you doing that?"

"Smoking tobacco?"

"I'm not stupid. You were smoking your card."

Lacy was quiet, watching the stars cross the ceiling. "A senior girl showed me," she said. "We were in her car with the sun coming in, everything beautiful, and she let me try hers. I watched the smoke in the sunlight, feeling good and clean with that cotton candy taste in my mouth. And suddenly, there were no programmed memories anymore, no false attachments, just this fuzzy cloud of electromagnetic energy rushing toward me, turning even my thoughts into pure crystal code. Then my toes curled and my jaw got so tight I had to pry my lips open just to laugh."

"That doesn't sound like fun," Joey said. "You're ruining your card."

"You can get two or three scrapes and they're still functional. Plus, I don't have to use mine. The popular girls are always getting upgrades. They throw theirs in the bathroom trash or sell them." Lacy had forgotten to pull the blinds closed, and the moonlight came in through the tree branches, casting shadows of leaves across her face.

"I don't like it," Joey said.

"Everything's fine," Lacy told him. "Just don't tell Mom or Dad."

So, when Joey saw Lacy's bloodshot eyes at dinner, he didn't tell their parents. And when he found her card, scraped raw and useless in the dresser drawer, he kept her secret. The houses on their block filled with ghosts and pumpkins, coffins and gravestones, and his mother took him to Halloween City, where he wanted a werewolf mask with a hairy snout and furry clawed hands. The costume, his mother told him, was too expensive. Look, she said, holding up a plastic bodysuit that was on sale, he could be Buzz Lightyear.

The Lightyear costume hung in his closet when she picked him up and drove them to his sister's school instead of home. Lacy wasn't in the principal's office when they arrived, but his father was, and the principal ushered Joey's parents into her office.

"You stay out there for a bit," Ms. Jones said to Joey. "I'll call you in a minute."

Joey already knew he disliked her. Adults were always forgetting how good his hearing was. He had teachers who punished the nonhumans in class when they got distracted by voices from adjacent classrooms. And though he'd told his teachers there was only so much he could do to turn down his inner volume, they always forgot. It was as if they couldn't be bothered to learn about his specifications. Everyone just pretended to treat him like another human kid, and by doing so they made him feel even more like a robot. Amid the clacking of the secretary's laptop keys, Joey closed his eyes, and listened to Ms. Jones through the wall. She was telling his parents that Lacy was at the nurse's, but he could see his sister's location blinking in his inner GPS. Her small light flashed blue in an empty classroom near the principal's office, letting him know she'd been put in sleep mode.

"Your daughter's in a lot of trouble," Ms. Jones told his parents. "We found her off campus in a car with three older kids smoking fluff."

"Fluff?" his mother asked. She admitted that Lacy had seemed out of sorts since tenth grade, but they'd figured it was a faulty emotion card and bought her a new one. They didn't know you could smoke them.

"It was explained in the email we sent at the beginning of the semester."

"I'm sorry," his father said. "We've been working a lot, we haven't been keeping the best track of emails."

"Well, I suggest you read them now. I know this is a surprise to you both, but I need you to understand what your daughter's involved in. Take a look at this."

Then there was silence, and though Joey listened carefully, he couldn't hear anything until his mother began to sob. "Would you like a tissue?" Ms. Jones asked.

"Why'd you show us that?" His father sounded scared.

"Because this addiction's brutal. It's not just their emotion cards, it's the glue in their bodies. The kids are scraping themselves to get high. The only sure way to get rid of the addiction is to buy a new model and start over."

"She's our daughter," his mother said.

"You can have the same daughter programmed, she'll look the same, talk the same, she just won't be addicted to—"

"We're not replacing her," his mother said.

"If you prefer, there's a program called Western Recovery in Colorado for kids like your daughter. The children are all emotion card free. She'll get to ride horses by Redstone cliffs. It's not cheap—room and board run about forty thousand—but she can have a second chance, hopefully clear the residues, and be able to return home one day."

"We can't afford that."

"Then the only other option is the Detroit detox clinic. It's for adults, but her warranty might cover part of the treatment. Look, I don't want to give you false hope—the boys Lacy was with spent two months at that clinic and they're already smoking again—but if you can keep her from getting access to cards long enough, there's a chance she can recover. I suggest you sign her up while she's on suspension. Monitor her closely, take away her phone, don't give her access to the internet, and change all your passwords. She was a good kid, and somewhere in there she still is, but she needs fixing. Honestly, a replacement is your best option."

Joey heard a chair scraping the floor, then the principal's footsteps.

"Joey?" she said, opening the door. "Come on in."

Joey sat down next to his mother. Outside the large picture window in Ms. Jones's office, a couple of high schoolers were making their way across the soccer field to the parking lot. There was a small boy walking on his own, his backpack heavy, his legs bending mechanically as he hurried away from the group of boys who were laughing and tossing pebbles at him.

"I called you in here," Ms. Jones said, "because I know you love your sister and want to protect her."

Joey nodded.

"Your sister was caught today doing drugs. Now, I'm going to ask you a question, and I need you to be honest with me—because there are times when it's easy to lie, and you'll hurt the people who you're trying to protect. You understand?"

Joey nodded again.

"Did you know your sister was smoking fluff?"

Joey wasn't sure how much dishonesty he was pro-grammed with, but when he opened his mouth, the word came out effortlessly. "No."

Ms. Jones let his answer hang in the silence. "You want to try that answer again?"

Joey shook his head.

"Okay then," Ms. Jones said, and extended a tablet across her desk toward Joey. "I think you need to see what can happen to your sister."

On the illuminated screen was a boy lying in bed. One of his fingers had been scraped down to the metal frame and he was gazing at the camera with a grin that reminded Joey of Lacy. His mother took the tablet from his hands and placed it back on the desk. "He doesn't need to see that."

"Yes he does. You all need to see what Lacy's headed for if she doesn't stop. This doesn't end well. Your daugh-ter's in trouble. And him," she said pointing at Joey. "He wants to protect his sister. But, Joey, you're not helping her right now. Your sister's already addicted. So, if you see her smoking, let your parents know. And if you see her with emotion cards, show your parents where she's hiding them. Understand?"

Joey lowered his eyes. "Okay," he said, though he didn't think it was as bad as the principal was making it. Lacy wasn't scraping her fingers raw. She'd gotten a new card at the start of October and had stayed happy for the whole month; she'd even helped spiderweb the bushes for Halloween.

"Is that everything?" Joey's father asked.

"That's all for now. She can come back on the fifteenth." His parents rose and Joey walked with them to the door. "Mr. and Mrs. Thompson," Ms. Jones said, "I know I sound cold, but I'm just trying to look out for all our children. Their families don't want their kids getting involved in what your daughter's got herself mixed up with. But I understand what you're going through. I had a daughter, too, same age as yours. She was also a sweet girl. All I can say is, I hope you have more luck than I did."

On the nights when his parents took Lacy to the detox sessions, Joey lay in the room alone, trying to separate real memories from the programmed ones. Lacy and him in the backyard digging for bugs and collecting them in a mason jar? Programmed. Lacy scraping her knee while they were taking turns with the skateboard? Real. Lacy hugging him that past summer, holding him close and telling him she loved him?

The rehab program sent Lacy home with sterilized week-long cards: pale-colored chips with no scrapable material. That first night she lay in bed and didn't talk about memories, just the sanitized topics programmed on each card. *Thanksgiving is coming soon, that'll be exciting. Have you heard about that poodle who went parachuting? The video has over eighty million hits.*

"She doesn't sound like Lacy anymore," his mother

complained. Couldn't they just get her an emotion card with a hundred percent honesty and sobriety? But that wasn't possible yet, the detox center told them. Sometimes it took months for children to adjust to sterilized cards. Lacy might not seem like herself, but they had to remember this was part of the detox process. She needed time to get the resins out of her. Until then, there were weekly cleaning sessions and installable downloads to help Lacy with her homework. It would all be fine if she'd just stick to the program.

But things weren't fine. Lacy was taking out her cards again. Joey saw the sterilized card on her bedside table, the tree limbs casting it in stripes of darkness.

"Joey?" she said to him one night. "We're still a team, right?" It was the first time she'd sounded like herself in weeks.

"Yeah, we're still a team."

"Well, that program I'm going to isn't helping."

"It's supposed to take time."

"I met someone nice at the program. He's older, and he's been through this stuff, he understands what I'm dealing with. He told me it's not safe to just quit smoking like I did. Really bad malfunctions can happen."

"Who is he?"

"Just a human who also smoked fluff. He lives with some other guys in Saline. They all know how to deal with recovery. He told me to contact him if I needed help, but I can't even text him for support. Mom and Dad took my phone away. Can I use yours?"

Lacy's eyes looked soft in the light, like he remembered from back when they still talked about pirates and X-Men movies. "You're not supposed to use a phone."

"I just want to text him to see if he can come talk to me. I'm hurting, I need friends. You're my brother, right? You'll help me, won't you?"

Joey reached down to where his clothes lay, found his pants, and shook out his phone. "Okay," he said, "but you have to give it back." And when, an hour later, she quietly opened her window and crawled onto the roof and down the oak tree, he didn't say anything—just watched as she got into the car at the end of the driveway and disappeared, far from the constellations that arced across the ceiling and far from his parents, who were waking him in the morning, asking where Lacy was, the sound of birdsong spilling into the room.

The police found her abandoned in a motel room along the state road to Saline. They brought her back that evening, and his parents took her into their arms while the cops advised they shut her down. That night, Joey heard his mother telling Lacy how much she meant to them. "Like so many people, your father and I couldn't have babies, but you're both our children," his mother said, inserting a sterilized card into Lacy's armpit. "Please, just stay in the program for us."

That night Lacy lay hollow-eyed, staring at the ceiling, and there were no conversations about anything at all, just the constellation lamp lighting their bodies in its cool glow. But when everyone was asleep, Lacy found where their parents had hidden the keys and stole the car, leaving it crashed in an abandoned neighborhood among burned-down houses. The police tracked her GPS, brought her back, and she escaped again. Their parents began to shut her down every evening at dusk, and she lay in bed silent and pale, as though she were broken. But during the day, when she was powered back on, she escaped while their parents were at work, taking their mother's jewelry with her. Their parents tracked her location, brought her home, placed another sterilized chip in her, but when she went missing again, Joey heard his parents through the wall.

"We don't have a choice, she's malfunctioning," his father said. "I don't want to do it either, but we have to think about Joey now."

"And leave her out there?"

His dad sighed heavily. "What else can we do? Shut her down every moment she's at home? Spend every night finding her, only to have her run away again?"

"It just feels heartless," his mother said.

"We can't help Lacy anymore. She's becoming dangerous to us all. And it's better than recycling her. Maybe out there she'll find some kind of help we can't provide."

And yet, Lacy's light sat blinking only a couple towns away, her GPS unmoving on Joey's inner map. It would be so easy to bring her home. He lay there watching Orion's constellation pass across the ceiling, return a third and fourth time, until his father was snoring. Then he pulled off his Avengers blanket, changed out of his pajamas, opened his window, and slipped down the oak tree and into the cab that was waiting at the end of the block.

Though it was late November, the front door of the ranch house was wide open. The lawn was strewn with plastic bags of garbage, pizza boxes, and a child's tricycle. Joey saw a man sitting at the kitchen table inside, working on something. What little light there was came from a lava lamp that filled the room with a mottled blue, sending shadows across the walls and momentarily illuminating a second man who was also sitting at the table, drinking a beer. Joey knocked on the screen door, and the man with the beer turned toward him.

"I'm looking for my sister."

It felt like forever before the man answered. "Come on in," he replied, and Joey stepped into the blue, underwater glow of the house, the screen door closing on its springs behind him. The other man had stopped working on whatever it was he had in front of him and turned to look at Joey.

"Her name's Lacy, her GPS says she's here," Joey said as he approached the men. Down the hallway, behind one of the closed doors, was the sound of a man coughing and the smell of burning plastic.

"I know," the man said, rising, and when he did, Joey saw the shotgun on the table. Alongside the gun were an assortment of amputated hands, the fingers scraped raw. The lava lamp sent blobs of purple light across the exposed wires and onto the armless torso of a boy no older than himself.

"Let's take you apart," the man said, grabbing Joey. "Where should we open him?"

The second man rose from the table with his shotgun and locked the front door. "Just wait. Matt'll be pissed if we scrape without telling him."

"Fuck Matt." He grabbed Joey more tightly. "This one just fell into our arms, it's ours."

"Matt pays the rent, I'm fucking telling him." The man lowered the shotgun at Joey. "Your sister's down that hallway. Come on, I'll show you." He pushed Joey ahead of him to the room at the end of the hall, then turned the knob and opened the door to the cotton candy stink.

The man leaning over his sister had a back so hairy it transformed the tattoos below his shoulders into dark, unrecognizable splotches. Lacy was lying motionless beneath him, covered by a thin white sheet, with her arm over her head and her emotion slot empty.

"The fuck you guys doing?" the guy said. Then he saw Joey and grinned. Lacy spasmed beneath the covers.

"Joey?" she said, pulling the sheet tightly over her body. "What are you doing here?"

Joey had practiced his speech on the drive over, a collection of all the real memories they'd ever shared: watching TV on the couch after school; a lightning storm crackling past their porch; paddle-boarding together at Pictured Rocks; the two of them playing chess—and though she'd won every game, she'd promised that next summer, if he beat her, she'd take him to Cedar Point, would sit next to him on the Raptor, said it would be okay, there was nothing to be scared of. But Joey hadn't been prepared for the men, or the guns, or the body parts, or his sister naked in bed, and all he could manage to say was "Can we go home now?"

For some reason this struck the man as incredibly funny. He rose from the bed with violent laughter, but Lacy grabbed his arm. "Matt, that's my brother, let him go."

"*Your brother?* He's a fucking score."

"He's not a fucking score. They'll trace him here."

"We're fine! The boys will burn his GPS in the backyard. That bot's got at least an ounce of fluff in him. He's not leaving here." Matt shrugged Lacy off and lumbered toward Joey, closing his hand around his shoulder tight enough to crush his frame. He put his fingers against Joey's face and pulled down the skin beneath his eyes. "You're fucking pristine," he said.

"Matt, you said you loved me. This is the only thing I'll ever ask, just let him go."

Matt turned toward Lacy and looked at her in the bed. Then he turned back to Joey, whose head was still in his grasp. "Nobody's letting anyone go. Come on," he said to Joey, "let's open you up."

That was when Joey heard the click of the safety. Lacy raised the gun from the bedside table and pointed it at Matt. "Let him go," she said.

Matt turned his head toward Lacy. *"Really?"* he asked. "You're going to shoot me for a fucking bot?"

"I can take a lot more bullets than you can," she said.

Joey looked to his sister. "Lacy—"

"Shut up, Joey. Matt, let him go. Now."

Matt released Joey from his grip and rose to face Lacy. "Don't pretend like you have emotions."

"Joey, leave. Right now. I'll be home soon, okay?"

And though Joey was certain he'd feel the men's hands pulling him back into the room, he listened to his sister, who was lying to him in the same breath as she was saving him. And Lacy was right: no one touched him as he ran down the hallway, or stopped him when he unlocked the front door and escaped into the waiting cab.

On the dark state road were farms and a couple of low-lying ranch houses. Every now and again a street lamp emerged, sending a momentary flash of light through the car. The driver adjusted his rearview mirror to look at Joey. "You okay?" he asked.

Joey was nestled in the corner of the backseat, looking out at the fields of dry and broken corn husks. Soon it'd be Christmas, and the radio station was playing some version of "Silent Night." What he needed was for his mother to hold him like she had when he was small. She'd wrapped him in her arms and covered him in his Snoopy

blanket and told him there was nothing to be afraid of—
no monsters in his closet, in the basement, or under his
bed. He was safe. And Joey realized, as clearly as if it were
his sister speaking, that none of those memories had ever
happened. There was no Snoopy blanket, no mom holding him, just the plastic flakes of another snow globe, and
his tears soaking the collar of his shirt against his chin.

"Hey, I'm sorry," the driver said. "It's none of my
business. I just got a brother who's in trouble is all, those
men reminded me of him. How about we listen to some
music. They're only playing Christmas songs, but it's
pretty all right."

Joey rolled down the window and felt the coldness of
the wind outside. Maybe tomorrow winter would come
and wouldn't leave for a long time. Tonight, when he
crawled through the window, the constellations would
move across Lacy's empty bed. He'd call the police, report
the house to them, and maybe they'd bring his sister back,
or arrest her, or find her in parts. But what did it matter?
She wasn't his sister anymore, just another model with
messed-up circuitry, trapped in a small room in a dark
ranch house in the Midwest, a robot who'd figured out
how to get past her own programming to become someone he didn't want to love anymore. And the little balloon
inside him expanded and deflated, expanded and deflated,
so full of pain he was certain it would pop.

Joey took his house keys from his pocket and reached
under his shirt, placed his fingers against the soft flesh

of his ribcage, and pushed the thin metal tab. When the cartridge released, his body grew cold, but there wasn't any pain anymore, just the chilling wind and a man driving, and the radio playing the tinny sound of Christmas music. And all this, Joey felt, was fine.

(SANCTUARY)

EARLY VISITATIONS

The first to stumble across the new lifeforms weren't NASA scientists or marine biologists, but a group of teenage gamers who posted their findings on GameShare. Their retweeted video arrived on our phones, looking like classic clickbait, but soon circulated every social media feed until even news stations were replaying the clip. We watched the recording and listened to the young boys' voices.

> *Any of you see that?*
> *See what?*
> *Down there, right side, past the cliff.*
> *Got it. All zombies dead.*
> *No, past the zombies—like on the side of the cliff.*
> *Whoa. What the hell?*
> *I don't know.*

Is that part of the game?

I don't think so.

Whoa!

Newscasters enlarged the image, and there it was, climbing through a rip in the fabric of the immersive game, as real as any living creature we'd ever seen. Its mouth snapped at the air with pincer-like teeth and the pixels around its body flickered with the prism of deep programming glitches. Yet, in interview after interview, programmers reported this wasn't an elaborate Easter egg nor a technological prank. "We don't know what *that thing* is," they said, looking pale and frightened. It sure didn't seem like they were lying.

Our own first encounters were in online offices, eClassrooms, and our immersive yoga studios. "Breathe in," our teacher instructed. We inhaled, stretched our arms above our heads, and listened to our avatar yogini. "Exhale, plant your hands, and move into chaturanga."

Indian fusion played in our ears, the sound of a sitar and tabla layered over a slow ebbing bass line, and we lowered ourselves onto the bamboo floor in the golden light of morning. Sunlight broke through the muslin curtains and something shimmered in the air, creating small waves in our vision. We readjusted our headsets, wondering if our system was glitching, but the console seemed fine.

"And stretch into downward dog," our teacher said, but we kept our eyes on the place where the room was bulging outward until, as though the studio was made of fabric, the air tore open and we gazed into the inky starriness speckled with planets, wondering if this was enlightenment.

It was then that an enormous green leg with small hairs and a chitinous shell pushed through the rip and stepped onto the bamboo floor. Another leg appeared, followed by a colossal mantis head which tore through the top of the gash. The creature's eyes were the size of dinner plates, and its segmented mouth emitted a series of high-pitched clicks as it examined us with insectile hunger. The instructor screamed and we fled from our yoga mats and ran toward the studio doors. Then, remembering we were online, we pulled the headsets from our eyes. We stood terrified in the safety of our small home offices, our IR consoles whirring quietly as we recalled how the creature had looked. It was almost as if *it* had been the frightened one.

SPECULATIONS

We assumed the creatures were nothing more than well-developed pranks, the kind of spam dreamed up by the technologically savvy to wreak havoc on our immersive worlds. And soon we received emailed apologies from our content providers confirming our assumptions. Everything, they assured us, was under control; the best of their IT departments were handling the glitches. For a couple of hours, a day at most, our movie streaming services, online games, and immersive environments would be shut down so they could find the virus and deprogram the bugs which were appearing across our landscapes.

Those of us attempting to log on to our meditation classes found *SITE NOT AVAILABLE* illuminated against the inside of our goggles. Our children, who'd paid for upgrades of cars, planes, and weapons, discovered blank screens instead. College classrooms were gone, as were our day-care centers and gyms. There was nothing but the darkness of our goggles and the blinking lights of our consoles.

That evening we listened to public statements from CEOs of all the major immersive corporations. They were dealing with a massive cyberattack, which as far as anyone could see had compromised every platform across the globe. They were still establishing attribution as they tackled this major breach and were certain they'd find the hackers hiding somewhere within the online labyrinth of VPN servers. We were not to reconnect or attempt to delete the bugs on our own.

But when our systems remained inoperative for over twenty-four hours, we turned to the blog posts emerging from Silicon Valley. The companies, it was rumored, had hired white hat hackers, who'd reached out to black hat hackers, who'd turned to the most nefarious code-crackers on the dark web for help. We sent emails, made angry phone calls, found the names of CEOs and searched them out on social media. What was going on, we wanted to know. When, we demanded, would our access be restored? And what were those creatures? RATs, worms, Trojan horses? Were the mantids a zombie army of bots, infecting our machines and using our consoles to do some evil hacker's bidding? Yet none of our guesses rang true. For if the glitches had been ransomware, where were the requests for our money? And if they were adware, why hadn't the creatures tried to sell us anything?

THE BLOSSOM FILES

It was then that the black hat hacker known as Scott Blossom appeared. He leaked internal memos of the largest corporations and shared the data mining done by their hired code-crackers. The companies, he told us, had gotten so desperate they'd reached out to third-world scammers, bitcoin miners, and dark-net thieves. All the while, their meticulously designed landscapes were being ruined by the presence of the insects. Here were images of giant grasshoppers amid Sega's Indy 500 games and enormous praying mantises materializing in immersive gyms. And then, Blossom revealed the truth: the bugs were some kind of extraterrestrial trapped within our immersive worlds—the most real thing in our unreal realities—and though the insects could interact with our coding, there were no traces of them in the programming, no data whatsoever.

The thrill of extraterrestrials filled us with nervous excitement. What planet had they come from? What intergalactic message would they deliver? Were we in

life-threatening danger? Amid all our questions hung
a shadow of guilt. We recalled the conference rooms
where we'd hurled office chairs at them, the online birthday parties where we'd grabbed our children, the college campuses where the creatures had clattered into the
classroom, clumsy as horses. We'd flung scalding coffee
at them and tried to cripple the enormous bugs with our
chairs, though they'd done nothing more than place their
front legs on our conference tables, their large antennae
frantically flickering as they suffered the digital objects
we'd hurled at them.

We wanted to see the creatures again. Our providers
had no right to deny us service. This miraculous event
wasn't their discovery to keep. We flooded phone lines
and filled inboxes. The most politically active surrounded
corporate offices with signs and bullhorns.

The CEO of a Buddhist meditation module was the
first to relent. He reopened his immersive monastery and
sent out an email extolling the ethos of an open web.
Soon other start-ups followed, then gaming companies,
then Google, then Apple, and finally our connections
flickered back to life and the protesters returned home to
place their goggles over their eyes.

The wounded creatures were still cowering in our
restaurants and conference rooms, and we approached
them cautiously. Wasn't it true that after mating female
mantises ripped the heads off their partners? Couldn't
they crush spines as easily as they did exoskeletons? We
worried they'd seize us in their front legs, stare at us with

their compound eyes, and press their abdomens to ours before tearing off our heads. But the creatures were no more dangerous than butterflies trapped in a glass, and as we gathered around them, they only stared at us, as if trying to determine whether we meant them harm.

SANCTUARY

Tasha Cozhani's piece first appeared in the *New York Times,* and later in our social media feeds, expanded upon thereafter by a thousand bloggers, corroborated by hundreds of scientists, and finally, voiced by one or two of our politicians. Cozhani was a professor of entomology at Cornell's immersive campus. She studied grasshoppers, aphids, and mantises, understood their migratory patterns, knew how their congregations acted when threatened. These creatures, she wrote, weren't the same as our own insects, though there were clear parallels. For one, instinctual reactions when traumatized. She referenced heart rates, swollen abdomens, ovipositor dysfunction. Immersive reality, Cozhani speculated, had been the intergalactic architecture through which we'd extended our communication tower to the cosmos, and our signal had been received. These creatures weren't coming to attack us, nor to invade or destroy; they were arriving, at our invitation, to seek sanctuary.

A group of entomologists from Prague corroborated Cozhani's theory, pointing to lacerations on wings, broken tibial spines, and cracked raptorial appendages. Not only were the insects highly intelligent but their intent was in no way malevolent. The creatures had been mistreated, they said, and seemed to have escaped from their own world to seek refuge in ours. They weren't hostile, nor were they the Antichrist as our religious leaders claimed; they'd simply arrived on our shores seeking something better.

"*Delusional*" was what AM talk-show hosts called Cozhani's theories. These insects were keepers of decay, squirming with stingers, neurotoxins, and poisonous mandibles. They were highly dangerous, anti-insect bloggers claimed. Their bodies hid viruses that would corrupt our immersive landscapes. An invasion of bugs destroying immersive reality was simply the start of a larger migration.

World leaders were in a panic. Already, more insects were appearing upon our virtual shores, floating through torn portals like boats emerging from the fog. But what was their message? They arrived with neither greetings of peace nor threats of war. They merely stood in our IR environments, their heads reaching the ceilings of our offices, staring at us with their silvery eyes as they chirped indecipherably. And soon we found ourselves in one of two camps: those who'd fed ants sugar crystals and watched them build tunnels in glass terrariums, and those who'd held magnifying glasses over their backs to watch them curl and incinerate under the sun's concentrated ray.

A Victoria's Secret store closed when two massive

grasshoppers appeared, pushing racks aside as they clattered through the aisles. A Carnival cruise had to refund payments when one of their immersive ocean liners became home to a dozen escaping mantids. A group of toddlers were terrified by a gigantic bleeding grasshopper that had appeared in their day-care center. And, finally, an Alabama county clerk named Frannie Sheffield had an anxiety attack when a praying mantis appeared at her office's immersive picnic. Her round face was broadcast on all the channels as she lay in her hospital bed, voicing the request of an increasing number of Americans. "Squash them," she said to the cameras.

It was a phrase soon chanted by others. They emerged in our communities with signs and T-shirts. "Squash them," they chanted outside the corporate offices of our immersive-content providers. The Fraternal Order of Police issued a unified statement condemning the interstellar creatures. Religious leaders quoted Bible verses about pestilence, infestations, and blights, and conservative talk show hosts gave inaccurate history lessons on the boll weevil. "What we need to do," a Georgia senator said, "is put up a firewall so powerful it'll roast those crickets." And finally, an immersive-home owner in Pendleton, Oregon, loaded a virtual shotgun and opened fire on the mantis that had emerged on the front lawn of his online home. We saw his face on the news stations the next day, the carcass of the creature behind him. "If the corporations aren't going to keep us safe," he said, "then it's up to us to defend ourselves."

THE OFFICIAL RESPONSE

The president appeared on our smartphones, and we took off our IR goggles and gathered to hear him. America, he announced, was under attack. The immersives had precipitated a national crisis that threatened our cities, our homes, and our way of life. And despite the claims of liberal media outlets, these creatures were neither docile nor here in peace. These bugs were intergalactic predators opening the doors of our immersive worlds in advance of even more horrific insects, and their appearance in our digital world was nothing more than a prelude to their invasion of our real one.

And yet, the president's fears didn't match reality. No giant mantises were emerging in our actual midst, nor were the creatures a danger to our children. They poked their heads peacefully into our infants' *Sesame Street* tutorials. Alongside Big Bird there now squatted an enormous grasshopper, and our immersive dance studios were becoming home to injured arrivals who wanted nothing more than food and water.

But the president had issued his executive order. A new immersive military was being formed. Online forces were ready to stop any creatures who attempted to crash our virtual borders. He praised the Pendleton shooter and urged our teenagers to turn their tanks from the war-torn landscapes of their video games toward the horizons which were dotted with insects. Blast the creatures with mortar shots, he said; use whatever resources you have to fight the aliens online. Then, facing the camera, he spoke the words we'd hoped never to hear.

"We are at war."

THE FIRST DAYS OF WAR

When we logged back on, we found our offices and universities swarming with white trucks and avatars in hazmat suits wrangling insects into refrigerated HGVs. A large van screeched to a halt in front of our yoga class and armed soldiers descended upon the mantis with projectile nets. The creature's thin antennae beat against the mesh, and it looked at us with its large black eyes. It raised its wings, frantically opening and closing them against the nets until we heard something crack.

"*Stop!*" we yelled. But the men, being men, didn't listen. They bashed us with nightsticks and corralled us into corners. They shot the creature with tranquilizers and pulled it across the pavement into their trucks. We stood on the stained bamboo floor, watching the vans disappear from our screens into some dark-web site where we couldn't follow. None of us felt like meditating anymore.

How many of them died in those early days, no one knows for sure. We demanded to know where the insects were being taken, but the president remained silent. Scott Blossom, who'd sought political asylum in Norway, leaked a video of cramped cages in an immersive detention center, the creatures mashed together within the wire pens as our president waged his war against the cosmos.

A group of black hat hackers arose in rebellion, programming temporary firewalls of safety which the government frantically sought to crash. The revolutionaries
appeared on our screens with insect masks and a video
of the enormous mantises they'd kept sheltered from
the roaming feds. "We're creating a worldwide network
of sanctuary sites," they announced. They spoke of
encrypted warehouses hidden deep within the inner cities
of our children's sandbox games, and of global protector-
ates scattered across the mountaintops of our skiing mod-
ules. It was up to us—hackers and everyday citizens—to
hide and protect the creatures.

There were many of us who'd never played video
games. We now lowered our goggles and sat with our ears
cradled in headsets as we fought our government, faced
firing squads, and respawned to fight again. Among the
new heroes were shop owners and schoolteachers, pas-
tors and firemen, mothers and fathers who hid grasshoppers in the basements of their online homes and offered
sanctuary within immersive churches and monasteries.

In response, we were bombarded by more invective
from the White House, praising the gamers who were
amassing insect casualties, and extolling the virtues of the
president's militiamen who were squashing the intruders
online. As for the traitors who would protect them, the
president announced he was sending real troops to kick in
the doors of the Silicon Valley offices that housed the black
hat anarchists. His hackers were already breaking through
our firewalls; they were coming for our sanctuary sites.

We attempted to herd the creatures back through the virtual rifts, but like crickets jumping away from an open door they refused to leave, resisting as if fighting death itself. They turned instead toward the open borders of our immersive worlds and cocked their heads, listening to the sound of the approaching tanks.

INTERGALACTIC SONGS

It was then that the creatures began to sing. The mantises, whose legs our doctors had mended, lifted their wings and rubbed them together, and their melodies rose above the gunfire with the sound of crickets on a summer evening. Their music reverberated across the rooftops of our blasted landscapes and set meditation bowls ringing, filling our bodies with a soft vibration that tasted like honey to our eardrums.

For a moment, we were awestruck by the beauty of their songs, which sounded almost like prayer. The citizens' brigades stopped marching, the dark-hearted gamers lowered their machine guns, and the tank operators idled in their war machines. Even those who at this late stage were still attempting to ignore the war and go shopping, paused and listened. The creatures' stridulations echoed from our sanctuary sites, a wave of exquisite music that was also a homing beacon to their hiding places. We tried to silence the creatures as they sang, but they just looked at us with their compound eyes and continued their melodies. The songs were beautiful, and for a moment we felt like children drawn to the glow of fireflies. Then, just as quickly as it had arisen, the spell was broken. The military trucks began to move again, the citizens began to march, the gunmen raised their controllers, and we finally understood a truth. Our visitors didn't need to tear us apart—we were doing that ourselves—and the distance they'd traveled was far less than the gulf between us and our own neighbors. Had we had more time, perhaps we could have learned their languages, translated their songs, understood the reasons they were here. But the tanks were already arriving. So we lifted our controllers, and faced our fellow humans.

(INFINITE REALITIES)

When we finally discovered the parallel timeline mouse, it was sleeping in a universe so onionskin close to our own that it existed in a parallel cage in a parallel lab where a parallel Donnie and I were doing similar parallel-timeline experiments. I isolated the mouse on my monitor and dragged its timeline onto our present one. Then Donnie and I looked at our mouse sipping water from the feeder.

"Okay, let's do it," Donnie said, and I hit Enter.

We waited, wondered if the Earth would stop spinning, if matter would crack open, if alternate timelines would go spilling across the universe. But none of that happened. Instead, the parallel-timeline mouse awoke inside the cage and sniffed his new universe. Then he crossed toward his present-timeline self and the two mice put their noses together. Did they know they were the same mouse simply overlapped from different timelines? Were they behaviorally different mice? Might this shed some light on the whole nature-versus-nurture debate? Who knew; we were opening the champagne.

Donnie had first asked if I could write programs for trans-dimensionality back in college. We'd been smoking some heavy-duty Indica, and I'd had a vision of a spider's web of infinite timelines, the program's layers as user-friendly as Photoshop. Yeah, I told him, I could do it, but he was the scientist—it was up to him to figure out the hard quantum shit, like traversing string theory and locating multiple realities. Sure enough, eight years later, he did.

We celebrated all week. Donnie splurged on expensive rum, and I broke out my top-shelf bud. We repeated experiments, recorded the transdimensional mouse, daydreamed about the Nobel Prize, and for a while it was high times in that lab. Donnie worked on wave/particle equations, leaving me to mess around with new programming. I worked to isolate anything we had biology on: a single strand of fur from Donnie's golden retriever let me track infinite parallel versions of his dog throughout the multiverse. Things were going great, but as we broke through the fabric of reality, all I could think about was Erin cheating on me with that woman at her stupid teachers' conference. I took bong hits after work and watched YouTube clips of cats riding skateboards to keep from dwelling on it.

We'd met at the campus Film Club three years earlier, and when I first saw Erin it was like we were two
alternate-timeline mice finally together in the same cage.
I invited her back to my place to smoke a bowl, and we
made out until early morning. By winter we were spending every day together, and by the end of the school year
she invited me to move into her apartment. It was tight,
but we made it work, pulling tubes and watching dumb
horror flicks late into the night. There wasn't room for
my equipment, so I worked on programming at the lab,
cracking the codes of time and space while Erin studied
education reform at home. Then her dissertation year
started and she stopped puffing altogether. I'd crawl into
bed after work, ready to tell her about our latest break-
through, but she'd just take my hand in hers, sniff it, and
tell me I better not touch her with my resin fingers. As if
that wasn't bad enough, after six months of no sex, she
went and cheated on me with some rando. So, yeah, I
was super bummed when I should've been celebrating the
mouse successes.

Erin was in bed reading when I came home from
the two hundredth lab test. I went into the kitchen and
looked for food but dinner was already cleaned up. "Any
leftovers?"

"Didn't make enough for two," she said, and looked
up. "Please tell me you didn't just walk into the kitchen
with your boots on."

"Shit, sorry." I took off my wet boots and put them
on the shoe rack, then grabbed some paper towels and

mopped up the muddy prints. I microwaved a burrito, which started another fight. Why did I eat junk all the time? Why did it matter if we weren't having sex? Maybe it'd be sexy if I got a job. Um, I had an actual job, I was doing groundbreaking freaking science. Playing with mice for two hundred bucks a week didn't constitute *groundbreaking science*. Well, maybe if she asked me about trans-dimensionality or spooky action at a distance she might know how freaking awesome our discoveries were. Was I seriously rolling a joint right now? Why the fuck not? Then she was shutting our bedroom door, and I was alone, puffing really good ganj out the kitchen window. I knocked on her door to ask if she wanted a hit, and she told me to start looking for a new apartment.

So, yeah, I was hurt and heartbroken. I wanted our old timeline back: a reality where we wrestled on the couch, made love every night, and when the munchies hit, bundled into parkas and trekked it to the Shell station for cheese puffs. And no, it wasn't morally right, or well-thought-out, or even a plan—I was just really high and had access to Erin's hair. Seriously, I wasn't trying to fuck up everyone's lives. I only wanted to know if somewhere in the universe there was an Erin who still loved me.

Among the nine million things that could've gone wrong: I could've wrecked the space-time continuum; the Earth could've become a black hole; the program could've glitched and an alternate Erin would've been trapped between parallel realities in a netherworld where particle trash and hungry ghosts passed her forever. But what I was hoping, when I dragged one of her timelines onto mine, was that particles would instinctively know how to make room for other particles, that a parallel-timeline concert was also happening at the Blind Pig, and that Erin would find herself there, seamlessly dancing, without ever knowing the difference. So I closed my eyes and hit Enter.

By the time I got to the club, Erin was by the stage. Her hair was longer and her shoulders weren't slumped from typing, and when she turned and saw me making my way through the crowd, I had that same fluttering feeling in my heart like the first time I'd seen her at the Film Club.

"Good band, huh?" I yelled.

"Ya!" she yelled back. "Did you see the first one?"

"No! It's loud in here!"

"Want to go smoke a bowl?"

"Sure!"

Alongside the other smokers, we got high in the alleyway for the first time in over a year. Erin told me about playing guitar in a dub-folk band and how she web-designed to pay the bills. I told her about the mouse experiments, and she didn't make fun of me. Instead she said, "Are you kidding? That's fucking incredible!" and looked at me with such curiosity that it was hard not to blush. I stared at the firebird tattoo on her neck instead; tattoos were something my timeline Erin hated. The bowl was cashed and she dug around in her pocket.

"Should've brought more," she said. "We can puff at my place if you want. It's in Chelsea, but I can give you a ride."

No you can't, I thought, looking at the garage across the street. "I have to finish an experiment tonight," I said. "How about tomorrow? Want to go for a walk at the arb?"

"I free up at four."

"Meet you by the gates?"

"It's a date," she said, and leaned forward, giving me a quick kiss, and the sudden softness of her mouth against mine was the most incredible feeling I'd had all year. I stood there, watching as she turned, thinking how there was a timeline where we were still in the alleyway making out, another where she was touring with a dub-folk band, and yet another where she'd soon leave the club and call the police about her missing car. *Shit.* I hurried back to the lab, highlighted her parallel self, and returned her to her own reality. Then I took out a pad and wrote down every detail I could remember: the sound of her voice, the warmth of her lips against mine, what it felt like to be wanted again. When I was done, I shut off the lights and went home to our apartment, where Erin was asleep, her own note on the kitchen table telling me to crash on the couch.

I hadn't expected to fall in love again so quickly. But at work the next day I told Donnie I needed to go home early, and before leaving I isolated the alternate Erin, dragged her timeline over my own, and hit Enter. Six hours later, we were parked outside the empty lab, making out in my car while snow came down heavy against the steamed-up windows. I let her into the building, showed her the mice, and finally highlighted her timeline and dragged her back over hers. We kissed one last time, the whole universe feeling alive, then I hit Enter and there was just me, alone in the lab with the small lights of my computer blinking and our two mice sleeping tightly against each other.

So I did what I knew had to happen in this reality. I called Donnie.

"*Are you totally insane?* Like fucking sociopathic?" Donnie asked when he arrived at the lab. He was still in pajama pants, his hair a mess, wearing a T-shirt with Einstein on it. "You brought another human into our reality?"

"Twice," I said.

"Do you have any fucking clue how dangerous that is?"

"Kinda."

"Kinda?" Donnie said. "*Kinda?* You could've imploded multiple realities."

"Precisely," I said. "Take a moment and process that. It worked!" And I kept reminding Donnie that the first human tests had worked, until he relaxed enough to stop panicking. I took the bottle of rum from the file cabinet and poured us two large tumblers while I told him about how Erin and I had walked together through the arb, the branches covered in a light dusting of snow, how the softness of her jacket had rubbed against mine, and her voice had been buoyant, how she was completely different from my Erin, who treated me as though I was an intruder in her joy.

"Can you speed up this story a bit? Like, to the part where you don't create an irreparable tear in time and space?"

"I'm just saying she was real in this universe. Like a perfect but better version of my Erin. She took the joint we were smoking from my hand as naturally as if we'd been together for years. Seriously, we should be celebrating."

"I'll celebrate once I know you haven't fucked up the multiverse," Donnie said. All the same, he took a long sip of his rum and sat down at his desk across from me.

"It was incredible," I told Donnie. "We were standing by the Huron River, the snow falling, her body buzzing against mine, sunlight making everything sparkly with winter, and she told me I was amazing. We kissed like it was the first time, the falling snow shimmering and beautiful around us."

"Wow, that's really fucking great, man. You risked imploding the universe for a make-out session with your girlfriend. Please tell me you didn't inform her she was from another reality."

"Well, I showed her the mouse video and told her *she* was the mouse and she freaked. 'You quantum kidnapped me?' she said. I tried to explain that the other her had cheated on me and we hadn't had sex for a year, but—"

"*Are you joking?*" Donnie said, and got up again. "That

means there's a person in another dimension who knows they've transcended realities."

"I figured it was the only right thing to do, especially since we were making out. But once she heard about the other her she demanded to see herself."

"*Fuck,*" Donnie said.

"Don't worry, they didn't meet. We just sat for a while in the car snooping on my place. It was getting dark and the snow was falling heavier, and Erin just watched my Erin as she worked on her computer. She wanted to know if she ever did anything else besides work on her dissertation, like play guitar, or smoke weed, or go to concerts. I told her she didn't. '*Shit, so I'm super lame in this reality,*' she said. Then she said she didn't want to mess with my Erin's head like I'd messed with hers, she just wanted to go back to her own universe."

I'd felt awful as I drove her back through downtown. I'd never meant to kidnap her or mess things up so badly. Ann Arbor was lit up with Christmas lights that hadn't been taken down yet, and it was super cozy and romantic with couples walking along Main Street holding hands. Erin was looking out her window at the guy on the corner wearing a wolf mask, playing violin in the falling snow.

"I still don't get it," she said. "If you were trying to get even with *her*, you could've cheated with someone in your own reality. Why'd you kidnap me?"

"Because I never thought of it as cheating," I said, "or kidnapping. I just thought of it as finding another part of you that still loved me in a subconscious string-theory kind of way. Seriously, I don't want anyone else, I only want you."

"Wait, she fucking bought that?" Donnie said.

"Bought what? It's the truth, I'm in love with her."

Which was what I'd told her in the car. We were stopped by a red light, with the pedestrians all passing, and she looked over at me and said, "Explain to me again why the other me isn't making out with you in this reality."

"I don't know," I said. "Maybe because I smoke too much weed?"

"Well, that's stupid. You should know that the other me is missing out because you're really hot," she said. And then we were kissing again, our hands all over each other, until the guy behind us was honking because the light had turned green.

"So, moral of the story is your girlfriend from another dimension thinks you're hot?" Donnie said.

"No, you're missing the point. Erin agreed with me. She said it was fucked up to make out together in a universe where the other her also existed, but that she'd be willing to keep seeing me if I came to her. Donnie, I can be the human test subject now. Put me in her timeline and bring me back. I'll give you reports. You know, for science."

"Uh-huh. Since when have you been remotely interested in the actual science of any of this?"

"I'm totally interested in science. Look, I took notes." I showed him my journal from the first meeting with Erin.

"What is this, a love letter?"'

"Look, you're the one who knows how to take lab notes. That's what I'm saying: Use me as your lab rat." And then, knowing the scientist in him could never say no, I added, "You *really* don't want to run tests?"

Donnie took a long drink of his rum before looking at me. "What if I can't bring you back?"

"That's not going to happen. You know how good my programs are. The experiment worked. The mice prove it, Erin proves it. This is what we wanted all along—the ability to travel through multiple dimensions. Seriously, we're talking about the Nobel Prize. Let's just try it, *for science's sake.*"

"Luke," Donnie said. He sat down across from me and tilted his glass in warning. "You're an incredible programmer, but sometimes you're also a fucking idiot. Maybe you were successful in our universe, but who knows what damage you caused in that other dimension. So, if we do this, you need to tell me everything from now on. No more lies about where you're going, no secrets. I'm going to need to know if anything in that world goes wrong."

"Of course." I clinked his glass. "Here's to infinite possibilities."

We started with a couple hours. Donnie dragged me over Erin's lake house, hit Enter, and suddenly the lab was gone and I was outside Erin's house in the cold. It had snowed in her reality and everything looked silvery and beautiful, the lake covered in a layer of snow, the branches all heavy with white. I walked to the front door, reached out and knocked, and there was Erin, opening the door in fuzzy slippers.

"I was wondering if you were coming. Well, welcome to my reality."

Erin's lake house was a one-bedroom cabin that had a living room with a sliding glass door to a porch overlooking the lake. On the floor by the window was a steaming cup of tea next to her guitar. I took off my shoes by the door, and Erin and I sat cross-legged on the warm wooden floor facing each other.

"I found the *other* you on Facebook." She held up my profile pic on her phone. There was my stupid cowlick, my jawline, my eyes, and my goofy smile. But this guy was way more buff and was standing beside a frizzy-haired woman and two boys who looked exactly like me. He was wearing a tank top that said "God Bless America."

"I look like I've never smoked a joint in my life."

"Want me to friend you?"

"Please don't."

"Check *this one* out." Erin swiped to an old photo of me at a weightlifting competition, my meaty hand on a beefcake dude, both of us giving a thumbs-up.

"Okay, that's super creepy."

"Kinda like if somebody grabbed you and put you in their timeline without asking?"

"I'm so sorry about that. Can you forgive me?"

"Yeah," Erin said, putting her phone away and placing

her hands against my thighs as she leaned toward me. "I think I can do that."

Donnie brought me back to the lab and I gave him notes on traversing timelines, let him take EKG readings and draw blood samples for interdimensional radioactivity. I asked him to increase my next visit to three hours, then five, and soon I was at Erin's lake house most of the day. We'd make love and smoke joints, and she'd practice new songs for me. There was no TV at the lake, so we did other things, like hiking and cooking and making plans to go kayaking once it got warmer. Being with her let me see how much of a slacker I'd been in my own universe. I envisioned that other me, slumped on the couch, my feet on the coffee table littered with roaches and beer bottles, playing video games all night, and I felt embarrassed for the person I'd become.

That evening when I returned to our small apartment, Erin was in the bedroom in front of her computer. I cleaned up the kitchen and did push-ups in the living room, and we didn't fight or argue about not having sex, I just surprised her by cooking dinner, and Erin was happy to have the time to write. She'd left her earrings on the kitchen table. They were a small gift I'd found at the Tibetan shop downtown when we first started dating—two turquoise teardrops. Seeing them, I suddenly envisioned a timeline where Erin was gone from my life, taking her earrings and everything else with her when she left.

"Hey," I said, standing in the doorway of our bedroom. Erin turned from the computer, annoyed, and I took a deep breath. "I know I've been smoking weed and playing video games all the time and probably haven't been that interesting to live with."

"Okay," she said.

"And I know you probably felt really alone because of it. And I'm sorry. I haven't been much of a boyfriend. I was hoping weed would help, because we used to laugh and have fun, but I was wrong. So, I just want you to know that I'd like to do other things with you, like take walks, or cook together, or . . . well . . . whatever you want to do. I just want to be with you."

Erin took a deep breath and looked at me. Then she got up and crossed the room and gave me a hug. I felt the warmth of her body against mine, and though I'd been holding her at the lake that afternoon, this Erin felt completely new.

"I'm glad you're saying this," she said into my ear, "but it's going to take time for me to believe you. I need to actually see you making changes."

And though we didn't kiss, just stood in the light of our bedroom, I could feel her love again, and when she let me go, instead of pulling tubes or turning on PlayStation, I decided to do some more push-ups in the living room and get into shape like that other me in Erin's world.

⚹

Things got better. I'd see Erin at the lake house during the day and spend evenings with the other Erin at night.

We cooked dinner at home and joked like we used to, and though we hadn't kissed yet, we hugged more. Meanwhile, in that other reality, Erin and I spent hours naked in bed pleasuring each other. Afterward, we lay together like new lovers, talking about a future where we'd use Donnie's discovery as a travel agency to teleport us to a multiverse in Paris or Morocco. But it was also true that life was getting complicated. Now that things were thawing at home, Erin was sending me romantic text messages that I couldn't answer for hours. I asked Donnie to field them for me.

"Sexting isn't in my job description," he said. "You know what is? Quantum physics research. You should try it sometime."

"Please. I'll write you notes you can use. Just text her back so she thinks I'm here."

And maybe everything could've worked out, the four of us functioning together across multiple dimensions— Donnie fielding texts for me, Erin and me happy at the lake house while the other us healed our past in the present— if only reality hadn't started getting weird. Like how Erin was humming a dub-folk melody while she worked on her thesis, the very same song the other Erin had been playing for me earlier that day. Or how she began talking about getting a tattoo, a firebird on her forearm. And then there was the night when she woke me. I was still sleeping on the couch, the moonlight coming through the living room window, and for a moment in my half-asleep state I thought I saw the frozen lake outside and couldn't remember whether I was at the lake house or our apartment.

"Luke?" Erin said from the doorway. I blinked my eyes and saw her guitar in the corner of the room.

"Yeah?" I said, rubbing my eyes.

"Can you come back to bed and hold me?"

So I got up from the couch, and there was no sliding glass doorway, no lake outside, no guitar in the corner, just the snowy windows of our small apartment, and our bedroom where I was finally being allowed back under the covers. I crawled beneath the blankets beside her, and Erin wrapped her arms around me.

"I had an awful dream," she said. "We were at this weird lake house smoking weed and we were so happy and in love, but you were cheating on me. I was playing this sad song for you on guitar, about the moon and my heart, and then you got up from bed and kissed me, and"—she started crying—"and I realized how much I've been missing you." She put her hand against my face.

"You dreamt about a lake house?"

"Luke," Erin said, wiping away her tears, "I'm sorry I cheated on you. I was sad and felt disconnected, and you didn't seem to notice, you were just smoking weed all the time, and I thought you were becoming someone different . . . and I didn't like the new you . . ."

"I understand," I said. "But what about the lake house in your dream?"

"Who cares, it was just a dumb house, that's not the

important part. What's important is the feeling I had of missing you and loving each other—I want that again."

"I want that, too," I said, and we kissed for what felt like the first time in over a year.

"Luke," she said, pulling away to look at me. "What's wrong? It's like you're somewhere else."

"I'm right here," I said.

"There's just this hollow feeling—it's awful. Like this morning, in class, I felt all this anger toward you, like you were cheating on me. Tell me the truth: Are you seeing someone else?"

"Just you," I said.

And then we were kissing again, our bodies warm against one another like the first time after the Film Club, her hands slipping beneath my shirt as we pulled each other's clothes off. "I haven't told you," Erin whispered, "but sometimes when you're at work, I can feel you touching me. Your lips against the back of my neck, your hands on me." She took my face and kissed me again. "I've been missing you so much. I'm sorry for what's been happening; I want us back." And we pressed our bodies together like we'd done at the lake house, the two of us feeling completely familiar and totally foreign from who we'd once been.

*

I knew I should mention Erin's dream to Donnie—it was the kind of thing he needed to know—but the next morning Erin and I woke up and made love again, and when she asked if I could skip work, I called Donnie and told him I'd be late.

Donnie was pissed when I got to the lab. "Dude, I don't know what's going on with you. First you complain about not having enough time in the parallel dimension, now you're showing up late? I need you *here,* we're totally falling behind on the mouse experiments." It was true. For all practical purposes, I'd been gone from the lab for weeks; progress on the next stage was slowing.

"Don't we need more data?" I asked.

"I've got tons of data. Seriously, you've got to stop messing around with your second girlfriend and get back to work."

"Oh, man," I said. "That's really going to mess things up for us." I sat there wondering if there was a reality where both Erins would fall in love and we could have a deeply meaningful threesome. I asked Donnie what he thought. "It'd be amazing, right? Though, I guess it might feel kind of narcissistic. Still, if you *didn't* want to hook up with yourself, does that mean you secretly have low self-esteem? What do you think? Would you ever make out with yourself?"

"Luke, what the fuck's wrong with you? I need you here in the lab with me to write new programs. We've got a serious situation on our hands. Have you even been reading the notes I left you about wave temporality and the dangers of collapsing timelines?"

"Um—"

"Okay, we're cutting you back to three hours."

Donnie was, of course, right, but mostly I was thinking about how hard it'd be not to see the other Erin. Plus, I knew I had to tell her about sleeping with this-reality Erin, but Erin just jumped on me when I appeared at the lake house, and we stripped each other naked and made love instead.

It was deep winter, the light already gone, and we lay in her bed, the candles flickering against the walls, watching the sun disappear behind the pines at the far end of the lake. Her hand was against my chest, her touch reminding me of all the mornings we'd woken up in bed together in our other reality, back when we'd find each other beneath the blankets, feeling as though we were the luckiest people alive.

"I've been feeling strange," Erin told me, her face highlighted by the glow of the candle. "It's like I'm living these two different lives that can never match up. I can't text, can't call, can only wait around for you to show up, and then you have to leave whenever your lab buddy calls you back. And meanwhile, the real you—the one in this reality—is just some married beefcake dude. What's that even mean? Is that secretly the real you?"

"No. This is the real me."

"Well, this setup sucks. I don't want you living with some other me, sleeping there, eating together; I want you here, with me, in my reality. You said you liked this me better, right? Can't you break up with that other me and move into my timeline?"

"Well . . . I mean . . . I've got my family in the other world, and my job."

"You could still visit them. Get a new job here."

I lay in bed wondering if that could work. Could I go back and visit my parents for the holidays, catch up with old buddies? And what about the other Erin, the one I had photos and memories of, the one who'd been sending me happy texts again, my lover who I was falling back in love with?

A small jewelry tree stood on the dresser, and hanging from it was the pair of turquoise earrings from the Tibetan shop that I'd bought Erin.

"Where'd you get those?" I asked. I got out of bed and looked at them. They had the same small fleck of tarnish in the silver, precisely the flaw in the pair I'd given Erin.

"Didn't you give me . . . Actually, let me see them," Erin said. I brought the earrings to her. "I can't remember where I got them, but they're really nice."

I didn't mention the earrings to Donnie when I got back to the lab, but that night I searched and couldn't find them anywhere. "Stop looking for things and come kiss me," Erin said, wrapping her arms around me. And though I wanted to double-check the bathroom cabinet, she pulled me into the bedroom where we made love again.

The next morning, Erin asked me about her favorite coffee mug. We'd gotten it a year ago when we drove cross-country to see her parents. "The one we got from

Montana with the big heart on it?" she said, rummaging through the cabinets.

I couldn't find it until that afternoon when I went to get water at the lake house and saw the mug in Erin's cabinet. "Do you recognize this?" I asked.

"Nope. Maybe somebody left it when I had a party."

I didn't say anything, but the next time I visited her, my PlayStation was in her living room. "Why'd you bring this?" she asked me. "I don't even have a TV."

I knew I had to tell Donnie what was happening, but I also knew if I did, he'd stop me from going back to Erin's reality altogether. I figured I could take my own notes, keep track of things for another couple weeks, figure out how to come clean with everyone, and maybe discover a happy solution for us all, but it was becoming harder to keep track of my timelines. In one reality I lay in bed with Erin, looking out our small window at the snowy street, remembering how we'd promised go kayaking, only to realize that wasn't in this reality at all. Next I was lying with Erin at the lake house, her room awash with the yellow glow of candlelight, and she was telling me about how she'd been getting interested in education reform, directly quoting passages from the dissertation my other Erin was working on. And then, late one afternoon, we were standing on her snow-dusted deck together, watching the light wane across the lake, and she was remembering the movie we'd seen on the night we'd met at the Film Club, a memory that was totally not hers.

A couple of geese were honking on the far side of the water, the first returns from their winter pilgrimage, and they floated along the defrosted edge, the sky darkening with evening. Somewhere, in another timeline, geese were probably returning to this same lake. Were they the same geese? Did they think the same goose thoughts? Was the lake house my future? That's when we heard the other Erin banging on the front door.

"Open this fucking door!"

"Who is that?" Erin said, turning from the lake and sliding open the glass.

"Luke! Erin! I know you're in there."

"Oh my god, that sounds like me," Erin said.

Then I was back in the lab looking at Donnie. "What the fuck, man?"

"Sorry," Donnie said. "She came by to surprise you and saw the sexting notes on my desk. I had to tell her the truth. She pretty much forced me to send her there."

"*What*? Put me back!"

"Listen," Donnie said. "This whole thing was not okay. Like not for science, or you, or Erin, or me—"

"Just send me back for a couple minutes so I can explain things."

"What's wrong with you? You cheated on two versions of your girlfriend. Neither of them is going to want to talk to you right now. You need to give them space. Go home, smoke dope, get some sleep, come back tomorrow."

What choice did I have? The moment I clicked Enter,

Donnie brought me right back to the lab. So, I walked home to our small apartment, where I could see traces of Erin in the moments before she'd left to surprise me. There was our bed, where last night we'd fantasized about a summer trip to Barcelona. There were the dishes from her lunch on the table, and drafts of her thesis by her computer—all glimpses of the life we'd been rebuilding before I'd ruined it. My PlayStation was gone, lost in an alternate dimension. All I had was some weed in the closet, and the six-pack I'd picked up on the way home. So I opened a bottle and loaded the bong for myself, and got high alone for the last time in what had once been our reality.

The door opened early next morning. I blinked awake, the whole world hurting, to find the two of them standing in the morning light looking like sisters. Lake House Erin surveyed our messy living room with the empty bottles, rolling papers, and ashy coffee table, then looked back at red-eyed, hungover me, seeing me for the first time the way my Erin had seen me for the past year. "Get out of bed," my Erin said before shutting the door behind her so I could get dressed.

When I finally sat across from the two Erins at the kitchen table, the world was swimming behind my eyes. "I can't believe you lied to me," Lake House Erin said and looked to the other her. "Last night I finally got to know myself, and I actually like who I am. I'm a good person,

Luke, and you helped me stab myself in the back." She reached out and put her hand on Erin's. "I'm sorry."

"It's not your fault; that's just what he does. He's selfish and fucked up," Erin said. Then she looked at me. "I was mad at you both, but now that I've had time alone with myself, I realize I'm just mad that I chose you again."

"But I love you. Isn't that, like, an even better testament of my love, that I love all the different versions of you?"

"Luke," my Erin said, "the only reason we're here is to tell you that this—us—is over."

"Can we talk about this? It doesn't have to end this way; there's infinite realities. What about the reality where all of us love one another?"

"We're going back to the lab," Erin said. "Erin's returning to her reality and I'm staying here in a reality without you. So take your clothes, take your fucking bong, and get your stuff out of here. When I get back, I want the front door locked with your key under the mat."

"Where am I supposed to go?"

"Some alternate dimension, a parallel universe, I don't care, just any reality that doesn't include me."

I looked to Lake House Erin. "I guess you were right about me coming to your reality."

"No way," she said. "You're manipulative, self-centered, and toxic, and you helped me lie to myself. That's seriously fucked up. I never want to see you again." Then she got up from the table, and I watched them leave the apartment, holding each other's hands as they disappeared from my reality forever.

I took a shower, my head still pounding. Then I gathered my clothes and packed a box with my video games and dope before calling Donnie to ask for help moving my stuff.

"Are you joking? I'm here with both Erins. They told me about the melding—the coffee mug, the earrings, your PlayStation—didn't you think that might be important? Like *crucial fucking information?* I can't help you move your shit, I'm a little busy trying to solve a quantum entanglement catastrophe that might implode reality."

"I'm sorry."

"*Sorry?* Dude, you were supposed to give me data, not lie to me so you could have sex with your alternate-reality girlfriend."

"I know. I'll do better in the future."

"Are you high? You're off the project. The passcode for the lab is changed, don't come back here." Then the connection went dead.

Everything Donnie had said was true: I'd betrayed our work together, betrayed our friendship, betrayed both Erins, broken the fabric of reality, and possibly fucked up the multiverse irreversibly; there was nothing to do but call my parents and tell them I needed a place to stay. And maybe it was at that moment when I finally saw clearly that the person I was in this timeline was just a self-centered, lying piece of crap who'd messed up everyone's reality, including my own.

In the end, Donnie was able to save our realities and fix the multiverse, and I moved back home and got a sales job at the Apple store. I saw Donnie on the news last Christmas, his video already gone viral, the two small mice meeting each other again, their pink noses touching. There was Donnie with his new assistant, a guy who looked exactly like me, just more clean-cut and trustworthy. The YouTube clip already has more than a billion views, and the world is soon going to become way more complicated. Maybe in a dozen years I'll have access to those programs I once wrote, and I'll be able to return to the night when I left our apartment drunk, stoned, and stupid enough to search for another Erin. I'll tell myself to go home, to stop smoking so much weed, and to try to fix our relationship instead. Who knows if I'll listen, but I can at least try. Because I know there are countless timelines where I'm someone good, parallel universes where I make the right choices and no one gets hurt, infinite realities where I'm a better human being. And maybe, if I try hard enough, one of those realities can also be this one.

MOUNTAIN SONG

That autumn, the robins and blue jays began filling walk-ways and roads, flapping aimlessly when I passed. They'd stopped building nests in the trees, and come October, the skies weren't filled with migrating geese. Instead, I watched them hang around our neighborhood for far too long. They began wandering cul-de-sacs and roaming in groups through shopping center parking lots as if searching for lost goslings. Specialists speculated the Towers were scrambling their internal compasses, but no one could say for sure. Then the storms came, the birds all froze, and the city removed them with the snow. It was heartbreaking, and if it weren't for urban avicultur-ists, raising doves and owls in underground aviaries, we'd have lost them all. But we seem to rise to the challenge in amazing ways. We avert doomsday visions, and the saviors keep birdsong alive for us. Still, it gives me pause, particularly when the humming throbs behind my eardrums, and I sense the interface inside me which has yet to fully open its eyes. It's nothing to worry about, I've told my parents. We're in the early stages; they're working on it.

⁙

Question: It's been almost two years since I talked to my parents. Is it right to still be angry at them?

Another parent question. It's pretty much all I get on my thinkstream now, ever since my thought-piece had its minor success. More than a hundred thousand users paid for my extended idea "Healing the Rift," and I got a lot of followers downloading my other thoughts.

"I know it's difficult to forgive right now," I think in response. "Our parents were binge drinkers of old tech. They put their microchips in everything and used us as guinea pigs. And yes they sobered up, became the worst kind of teetotalers imaginable, and nearly destroyed America. But China lost, we won, and our generation is leading the way. Do your best to be compassionate, our parents are processing their defeat," I think, feeling like a hypocrite. I have over a hundred unanswered thoughts from my parents in my memory. "For now, take a long hard look at yourself and find a way to open your heart again."

I think *Read* and my inner voice repeats my sentences inside my head. Everything sounds fine until I hear *Take the long cart look at your elf*. I bring up thought-to-text and fix it manually. If you don't catch autocorrect you end up with a whole lot of *WTF*s and no accepted advice. I make my answer available on the thinkstream and within the hour I've gotten fifty-seven purchases. It's not bad, though my ideas have been dwindling since "Healing the Rift" spawned a thousand copycat thinkers.

What I should've done was gotten licensed as a Tower technician. For a short, gold-rush moment, there were massive digging projects, Tower-construction jobs, and swaths of terrestrial data-blasting on US soil again. Half a million new jobs in the Midwest alone. Then tech speculators laid claims before any of us knew our minds were something to privatize. They purchased the beachfront property of our inner thoughts, installed frontal-lobe games, inner-ear jingles, stream-of-consciousness feeds, and mined the unexplored caves of our unconscious mind, making millions from our uncopyrighted fantasies. Meanwhile, I'm not dreaming up any mind games or ways to stream better sex, I'm just hoping to have enough good advice to be able to pay rent.

It's two a.m. when I finally rise from my couch and crawl into bed. I lie there counting the repetitions of the humming, my body pulsing with the electronic heartbeat that sounds from across the dead plains. *Arum, rum, rum; arum, rum, rum; arum, rum, rum.* I think of a car alarm, so far away all you can hear is its muted echo. It ebbs and flows, then recedes for a minute, leaving me with a couple glorious seconds of quiet. My eyes grow heavy, and for a moment I dream. I see shapes, neon octagons, black pyramids; a fox darts across my vision. *Arum, rum, rum; arum, rum, rum; arum, rum, rum.* The fox raises its head, the shapes tremble and fade, I open my eyes. It's just me: awake.

Last month, after I'd gone two weeks without sleep, I finally broke down and downloaded a white-noise app to run behind my thoughts. The 432 Hz vibration helps replenish DNA and allows you to work longer without sleep. It came with a free deep-meditation trial as well, which guided me through a series of breathing exercises and put me into a REM-like state. If I had spare funds, I would've kept it, but the free trial ran out and now all I have access to are short mindfulness clips. I play a two-minute sample called Deep Rest.

"Relax," the voice within me says. "Let everything grow heavy, as if your body is sinking into a warm bath. Let your breath relax your toes." Within my mind, the Icelandic Northern Lights glimmer with green dust and I hear the sound of a waterfall plummeting hundreds of feet to a pool below, the immersion so real I can almost taste the mist on my tongue. There's the swirling darkness of sleep, the tug of the dreamworld on the horizon.

"Hey! Did you know girls like me are ready to play in your inner vision?" an eighteen-year-old cheerleader wearing a low-cut top asks me. She waves to me in my mind's eye. "Come play with me! I'm ready!" I try to breathe into my toes, but she just leans forward, showing me her breasts, and blows a seductive kiss. The pop-up disappears, and I'm back to the last minute of the sample meditation. "Breathe into the soles of your feet—"

I shut down the guru, get out of bed, and slide open the double glass of my bedroom window. There's the sound of cars on the freeway, the buzz of our security lights, and over the peaks of neighboring apartment buildings, the Towers humming amid the cornfields.

When I was a kid, you could hear the Rockies singing at night. There were birds settling on branches, bugs scurrying along the ground, the footfalls of black bears, and the trickle of melting snow. I'd lie there listening to the sounds and fall asleep without ever knowing I'd closed my eyes. Nights like these, I try to remember what the mountains sounded like, soft and quiet, but it's hard. Mostly I just remember the rattle of trucks and the explosions when my father took me to see the mining. He pulled to the side of the road and we looked out at the yellow machines splattered with mud, the blasted rock, and the slurry pits filled with runoff. "It's over," he said. Soon after, he sold our house to the coal company and we moved east to Ohio, where at least the land was naturally flat. He took a job monitoring remote rigs, which seemed like the most boring job ever. I'd see him sitting in his bodysuit in his office, his goggles down, his monitor showing the dark interstate somewhere out west. There were stars and the high beams of the truck he was watching, and nothing for my father to do except monitor the navigation. Not once in all those years was he actually needed, not to dodge a drunk driver or slow the vehicle to avoid hitting a deer, not to pump the brakes for a pedestrian or pick up a hitchhiker. It was just him, listening to the road through his headphones and watching the endless drives all day and night. Sometimes I think it was that job that blunted his hope for the future and helped him feel okay about destroying mine.

I try to imagine the sound of the Rockies but it doesn't work. It's four a.m., my head aches, my fingers are jittery, and my lips feel dry and cracked, so I take sleep meds, even though I've been taking them way too often. The meds drown out the throbbing, though my sleep is spotty. I have delusional, half-awake dreams of fiber-optic cables, thin as spiderwebs, reaching from the Towers to the powders inside my pills. Thought-bloggers claim that deep within Synapse's endless user agreement is our approval for mining REM brain waves, but the idea that the Towers are raiding our memories while we sleep is a bit too paranoid for me.

I close my eyes, feel the grogginess from the pills dissolving, and end up dreaming about my parents again. We're on the back deck that I helped paint when I was a kid. Dad's showing me how to strip the old flaking paint and sand it down, the dust rising around us in the early summer light. There's the crisp smell of Rocky pines, the deck warming with morning, the cool night air evaporating in a mist around us. My father's face is freckled with paint chips, the sunlight behind him highlighting the deck, everything feeling good until I feel the wires within the sunbeams: a thousand tiny strands entering my eyes, pulling memories from me into the glowing sun above with a sickly popping sound.

I awake from the nightmare to an incoming suggestion. *How about some words from inspirational leaders to lighten your mood?* Synapse asks.

I agree, listen to a powerful speech on inner freedom by Nelson Mandela, and I even tear up a little, but mostly because Mandela's world was so unlike ours. The peaks of South Africa are gone, the Rockies too. Two years ago, when a job for a Tower technician opened in Denver, I flew out for the interview and saw the brown expanse of earth where the mountains used to be. One low peak that hadn't yet been removed rose like a mistake. I rented a car, went to the interview, and tried to visit my hometown, but the old mining-company fences stretched for miles. I drove and drove but couldn't find any way in. Finally, I stopped at a Conoco station, where the kid working the pumps told me the only entrance was two hundred miles north.

"You looking for mining work?" he asked. "Coal's all gone."

"I just want to see Lyons again," I said.

He looked at me in the dim station lights. "There aren't any lions behind that fence."

Question: You ever wonder what we missed during all those years? Ever feel like our parents owe us for them?

"I know this might sound clichéd," I think as I drive toward my parents' house, "but our parents don't *owe us*. They gave birth to us, they raised us, and yes, they made serious mistakes. But our work is to focus on the present and build the future. It's our generation, our technology, our victory." I post the answer, make it available for purchase, but it's not very popular. As for my actual feelings about the issue? *They fucking robbed us.*

My generation grew up with a famine of information. Our high school years were monitored by foreign gatekeepers. The photos we posted were screened, edited, and censored. Landlines came back. AM radio became our streaming service. Letters were the only reliable form of uncensored information. And for a frightening five years it seemed as though the US would become nothing more than a newly acquired Chinese province. Thank god our hackers fought the broadband wars, destroyed satellites, code-cracked the Chinese-bought senators, and wrestled back control of the government to finally impeach our thought-corrupted president. And once my generation had control, we built the new towers.

Yes, maybe the birds are dying and my sleep is haunted, but America will never be controlled again. No spectrum-throttling, no paid pre-authorization, no thousand-dollar VPN server access, but non-localized broadband consciousness and full-spectrum connectivity available to everyone. That's what true democracy looks like: access at all times, no one denied or able to turn off anyone else's screens, the internet as free and open as unsettled territory.

This is the one-sided argument I have on the drive to my parents' place. It's been a long time since I've talked to them. The last conversation we had was an ugly thought-battle between my father and me about the Towers. Still, I reached out last month, because I can't stand being a hypocrite, and like I advise others: You have to give your parents the chance to apologize.

"I've been trying to reach you for over a year," my dad said when I thought-messaged him.

"Well, you're seeing me now." I watched him grimace in my mind's eye.

"Come have dinner with us. We need to talk."

"Can't we just think-chat and eat dinner separately the normal way? For real, it's a long drive to you guys."

"It's an hour. Come to dinner, Mom really needs to see you."

So I gave in, even though driving makes my eyes heavy. It's a boring ride. All of the Midwest looks the same. We lost Nebraska to the droughts, then Iowa, then Kansas, then Missouri. Last summer left Michigan as barren as Colorado. Now all we have are canyons where the Great Lakes once were, dusty brown lawns, and swaths of cracking cornfield. At least the winter lets the dust settle and turns the air sharp and crisp, reminding me of what good air is supposed to taste like.

I try my best to stay awake during the drive by blasting

songs in my head. I roll down my windows and spike my adrenaline by mentally preparing for the Tower argument I know my dad will want to have. To be fair, my parents were freaked. In fifth grade, Tommy Sotto's chip misfired and he started glitching at the back of class. There were the cancer scares, the smart-car crashes, the hacked pets, then the voting hijacking, and suddenly my parents' generation did an about-face. They imposed sanctions, chained the FCC, and hobbled innovation. We watched month-long congressional hearings on TV instead of investing in technology. And what did we get from their stalling? China. But even this argument doesn't keep me from closing my eyes while I drive. Eventually, I pull into a gas station, pay for another meditation download, and try to get some rest.

I still feel like a zombie when I arrive at my parents' place. Dinner goes pretty much how I expected. My dad keeps putting down my job, telling me there's no future in advice slinging, but I'm so sleepy that his voice just sounds like waves, the air rippling with his words.

"Have some more potatoes," my mother says, passing me the dish. "Russets are on sale at Kroger's—five pounds for fifty dollars."

"Thanks," I say and take the plate heaped with soft white mashers. I imagine placing my head in them and sleeping. "Dad," I yawn, rubbing my eyes, "things are good. My job pays for my apartment and food. Maybe it's not perfect but—"

"Have you been listening to a single thing I've said? You need to move away from here."

"Are you a summer person or a winter person?" my mother asks me.

"There are places in South America where expats are settling," my dad says, ignoring her.

"You're kidding, right? I'm not moving to South America."

"Listen to me," my father says. "You need to go while you still can. The water's gone, the air is going, the birds are dying, there are no jobs left, and—"

"*Dad*, stop being so gloom-and-doom. Things are getting better. In African villages, kids who never would've had access to a college education are watching fully immersive neurosurgery tutorials behind their closed eyes. Feminist literature is being streamed into the minds of girls who've been kept illiterate, and we're offering jobs to millions of people in the third world who can now produce clothing at a virtual distance while never having to work in the sweatshop factories of your era."

"Would you say you're a dog person or a cat person?" my mother asks me.

"Mom, why are you asking—"

"That's not progress," my father says. "All your wonderful Towers did was open up a market of children who work for even less than they made before. They're not liberated. Their minds are their new sweatshops."

I yawn. I can hear my dad still speaking, but it's like

listening from a great distance, and though I try to focus, it's no use. I can sense the world of dreams hanging within reach, a curtain that simply needs parting. The fork drops from my hand and clatters against the plate.

"Sorry," I say and open my eyes.

"Evan, are you okay?" Dad asks.

"I'm tired."

"So then you'd say you're a night owl rather than an early-morning riser?"

"Mom, what are you talking about?"

My father puts his hand on hers. "Honey, isn't there cake? You could serve that now, right?"

Mom gets up to go cut it.

"What's up with Mom?" I ask when she's out of the room. From the kitchen, we hear her humming a pop-up jingle.

"Your technology is what's up with Mom. She's been asking me the same questions. Some insta-quiz that's leaking into her brain."

"Why doesn't she just focus away from it?"

"How? You want to tell me that, Evan? What about taking some time to sit with her and helping her understand how to deal with this new technology you've put in her head? I messaged you a thousand times, but you never answer."

"I was busy with work. Besides, it's not that hard. Just focus on the thoughts you want."

"Do you have any clue how difficult it is to control this at our age?" He motions to his head. "I paid someone your age to come talk with Mom. You know what he did? He taught her how to play Thoughts with Friends. Now she sits up at night sharing her stream of consciousness with completely random people who send her ads for fantasy vacations. I try to tell her to rest, but neither of us can sleep. Every night I'm filtering through a thousand thoughts about specials on prescription meds, women I don't want to talk to, consciousness-server updates, and mindless chats. I can barely keep my thoughts focused right now to have this conversation with you because there is a half-naked woman in my mind trying to sell me GRE prep tests."

"Dad, you just need to spend some more time controlling your thoughts. I could show you some basic things, but it'd be a thousand times easier to download a thought tutorial."

"Listen to me. We're leaving. That's what I've wanted to tell you for the last half a year. Your mom needs her mind back, and I need peace and quiet. We want you to come with us. I'll pay for your plane ticket, you just need to make sure your passport is current."

"What do you mean you're leaving? Where are you going?"

"Peru," he says. "The last of the Andes are still standing. There's a place where the Towers haven't reached. We don't have much left, but the house is on the market and we got a bid last week. It's not a great bid, but it's enough to get us all down there and live for a couple of years."

"And do what?"

"Survive," my father says, and my mother arrives,

humming a dating-site jingle, bringing chocolate cake for us all.

⁎

When dessert's finished, my parents walk me to the door and we hug goodbye. It feels weird to actually touch them again instead of thought-embracing. My father puts his hand on my shoulder, his breath condensing in the cold night. "Come with us," he says.

The snow has started falling, the flakes landing against our jackets. "I'm cold, Dad. I'm going to go."

"Please," he says again. "Tell me you'll consider it. I'll reach out to you soon, just actually listen to my thoughts." My mom starts with her quiz questions again, so I promise I'll consider it. And then, before either of them can say anything else, I start up my car, put it in reverse, and pull out of the driveway, watching my parents stand there, waving a last time before they're gone.

The freeway is barely alive. Only a single driverless truck barrels past in the darkness, disappearing into the distance. I watch its taillights growing dimmer through the falling snow, knowing that somewhere in India there's a father sitting in a dark, empty room, think-monitoring the truck's journey. What I tell myself is that things are going to get better. They'll fix the problems, Mom will recover, my folks won't have to disappear into the mountains of Peru to escape progress. How long do they even think it'll be before the Towers arrive? There are more satellites going up daily. They'll have a year, maybe two at most. I envision them living out of a microbus by the foothills, washing their clothes in the river, rising with the sun, wind drumming, *arum, rum, rum; arum, rum, rum; arum, rum, rum.* I'm drifting to the side of the road. I shake my head awake, roll down the window so the flurries whip in, and signal to get off the interstate for the safety of local roads. Far ahead on the horizon, a Tower reaches into the sky, and for a moment I imagine it lifting off like a rocket, heading past the clouds, up through our stratosphere, drawn toward the satellites floating high above, *arum, rum, rum; arum, rum, rum; arum, rum, rum.* The sharp beams of a hatchback startle me at the intersection of the exit ramp. I slow down, let it pass, and watch its taillights on the road as I pull behind it. Up ahead, another car merges onto our road, then another. A pickup truck appears behind me, until I'm in a line of cars, all of us creeping along the state road like some long metallic caterpillar, closing the distance between us and the Tower that squats in the middle of the dead fields.

It's when we come over a small hill that I see the horde of mismatched automobiles at the Tower's base, their parking lights speckled across the dark field like fireflies. There's an old Tesla, a sedan and a minivan, and a dozen other cars huffing exhaust into the darkness. The hatchback in front of me slows to a crawl, signals, and pulls into the frozen soybean fields. I take my foot off the gas and almost come to a stop in the middle of the road, watching, until the lights of the car behind me flood my cabin with high beams, and then I pull off the road, too.

The snow is coming down heavy now, settling against the roofs of the cars as I park next to the hatchback. There's the sleepy sound of another car arriving, its low beams cutting through the dark as it approaches the community camped here by the Towers, and when I hear its engine, I become aware of the silence. The base of the Tower is a dead spot, maybe the only place free from the never-ending drone. There's no humming, no constant thrum within my head, no incoming messages or pop-up thoughts to block; there's just the purr of car engines and the quiet of falling snow.

I turn off my headlights and watch the flow of arriving cars illuminating the winter storm. I have no clue if parking here is legal or if the cops will soon arrive to arrest us. Maybe the farmer whose ground this Tower squats on has been given permission for the good of us all. Or maybe the police are here with their own families, slumbering behind the foggy windows of their four-door wagons. I want to message Dad, to tell him to bring Mom, but there's no connection for me to send a thought, and besides, I can already feel it so clearly: in a moment I'll be dreaming.

With my eyes closed, I envision the mountains rising high behind my childhood home, full of earth and pine, crisp with the cold of winter. Soon we'll sand the porch down, open the buckets of paint, dip our brushes in. But for now, there's the splintery green of the deck and perched on the edge of the railing a single cardinal trying to sing. If it sings just right, it'll bring the mountains back.

They'll rise around us, the earth splitting with their peaks, as the cardinal's melody pulls foothills from the soil like worms. *Mom,* I start to say, but no words come to my lips. Just the cardinal's head growing larger in my vision, its breast rising as it opens its beak to let out a note, and I open my mouth along with it, my voice cracking with song.

(ISLANDERS)

We're getting suited up in the purple light. It's so dark I can just make out the water's edge where an old rusted yield sign rises from the waves like a shark's fin. Along the horizon, the clouds are streaked with a thin band of sky that promises sun. I squish into the cold rubber of my wetsuit in the darkness. Dad leans against the truck, the gray smoke of his pre-dive cigarette blue in the twilight as he looks out at the sea. There's a photo from before I was born, when he and Mom were still together: Dad's on the porch of our house, one hand resting on the deck railing while his other holds a cigarette like he's about to take a drag. He's looking at something off camera, and whatever he's looking at is making him happy. He has that same relaxed look now, staring out at the water, the waves against the concrete making a soft puckering sound.

"All right, let's dive," he says, tossing his cigarette into the water, where it goes out with a hiss. I heft on my tank and Dad puts on his. We check our gauges, squeeze into our flippers, lower our goggles, and go waddling backward toward the end of the street where the concrete slopes under the water, until I feel the ocean around me and I kick off, leaving the safety of land behind.

Everything is quiet, just the swoosh of the air tank and the sun breaking through the clouds for one brief second, lighting up the sea in golden streaks. A school of minnows swims past, silver as they turn in the light, and the rays reach below to the ranch houses of our old neighborhood, their vinyl siding swaying in the current like loose Band-Aids. We dive past the apartment complex where Mom lived after she left us, and on toward the elementary school where a couple of bluefish swim from the school's open doors. Dad paddles through the entrance, his diving light flickering across the lockers, and I can't figure out why we're here. We already salvaged all the usable supplies: pencils and pens which didn't work well, and a bunch of notebooks we laid out in the living room until the pages dried all crinkled and sea-stained. Dad cracks one of the rusted locks with the butt of his flashlight and opens the locker to reveal the bloated sleeve of a puffy jacket, too small to fit me. All the same, he stuffs it into the net, along with a textbook, which is already falling apart. I want to ask him what I need an elementary math book for, but before I can tap his shoulder he's kicking off down the dark, sandy hallway and out through the back exit.

We dive past the grocery store with its looted aisles and rusted shopping carts, over to the tall brownstones where conchs cling to the waterlogged plush of sofas and hold tight to the walls. Dad and I take out our knives, slice their grip and drop them into the nets, taking a good haul. There's a machine on a bookshelf that Dad stuffs into the mesh alongside the winter coat, and I wonder if he's getting worse. Sometimes I think he's doing fine, but then I'll find him sitting outside in the rain, his clothes soaked, and I've got to take him back in and heat up tea because he's shivering. Dad starts pulling at the objects beneath where the machine sat and their paper covers come apart like fish food. Maybe his mind really is gone, and he's envisioning those black round discs he's stuffing into the net as flounder, the puffy jacket as the arms of an octopus.

I fill my bag with conchs, probably a haul of twenty before Dad flashes his light on me and we kick off, leaving the submerged neighborhood behind with its lawns of seagrass and eels. Then we follow the road as it curves uphill until finally the ground is beneath our flippers again, and we walk backward from the water, our tanks heavy with gravity.

I sit down on the truck's flatbed and strip out of my diving suit in the spitting rain. Out over the ocean there's still that thin patch in the clouds where you can almost see blue. Maybe this is the start, I think. Maybe the rains are ending. But I always think that, and it never happens.

Dad lifts our haul into the back of the truck. "Why'd you take all that stuff?" I ask. He doesn't answer, just pulls a pack of cigarettes from the dash and lights one. Then he bungees the tanks into the back, and I feel the fat drops against my face, the incoming storm already drumming onto the roof of the cab.

"Time to head home," Dad says and starts up the truck, leaving me with all my unanswered questions, just like he always does.

The storms are back with the sound of thunder and sheets of rain coming down against the windows of what used to be our sunroom. Dad's sitting at a card table out there in the dark, hunched over the machine he pulled from the sea. He's got the oil lamp next to him and he stoops his head in the small circle of light, looking like he's in the hull of a submarine. It's getting late and we should eat soon, but Dad doesn't look like he's even thinking about cooking. He's got his screwdriver and is working the screws out one by one, and I try to imagine myself at his age, alone in this house on a hill that's barely above water, messing with some waterlogged machine. All I see is me in our sailboat trying to go someplace far from here, out across the waves where my mother and the other survivors went.

Back before our town disappeared beneath the ocean, there were other families in the neighborhood with kids who went away to college. There were architecture programs, and I imagined one day I'd move to New York and learn how to build skyscrapers. That was before that city also disappeared beneath the ocean.

"Why don't we sail someplace," I used to ask Dad. "There's got to be other people across the waves. Mom might still be alive."

"Sure, there are people out there," Dad said. "Whole cities above the waterline, and plenty of islands wherever the elevation's high enough. But I know what humans are like when they're hungry, and I know what the government's like, and I also know what your mom was like. If she's still alive, she doesn't want to see us. But we have it good here, you and me. We can fish, we can dive, we can make it through this storm however long it lasts. And when the waters recede we're going to have a windfall of land that'll be ours. Don't worry, we'll make it through."

Eventually I stopped asking about leaving, just let him tell me what to do, as though he still thinks I'm a kid he has to save from the incoming tide. This is how you collect drinking water from the rain. This is how to boil seawater to get salt. This is how you make the wood burn slower. This is how you sail, even though the sailboat he built has been sitting in our barn, abandoned and useless, for years. Sometimes I'll go out there when Dad's asleep, sit on the deck as it rocks on the tide. That sailboat was supposed to be our escape when the waters reached our doorstep—big enough for our whole family—but then Mom left, and the waters only came as far as the barn, and

I was abandoned here, gutting fish and scaling them off our porch in the rain, wondering if this is what the rest of my life will look like.

"What is that?" I ask when I bring the shelled conchs inside. Dad doesn't answer, just pulls the lamp closer to the machine, works at a stuck screw, the sound of rain crashing in waves against the house.

"Come hold the bottom," he says. And when I do, he lifts the top out like pulling meat from a lobster. There's a whole mess of corroded wires hanging from the piece he's holding, their ends dripping seawater into the case. "Go ahead and dump that water outside."

I cross the room, the salt water sloshing in the container, and bend down to put it on the floor before opening the front door. The rain splatters my arms with cold when I open it, and Dad finally answers my question.

"It's called a turntable—plays music," he says. "Your mom and I used to like listening to records." I don't move, afraid if I dump the water he'll stop talking, but maybe if I keep the door open to the wind and the rain he'll say more about what she was like, where she might be, if he thinks she misses me.

"What kind of music did she like?"

"Shut the door," he says. "You're letting the rain in." And though I want him to keep talking about Mom, he doesn't, just places the machine back in the case when I bring it to him and gently pries off the center ring at the middle of the disc to reveal another set of screws.

"Funny how you forget names," he finally says.

"Lightning Hopkins, Nina Simone, James Brown, Mississippi John Hurt . . ." He places a screw in a small dish and starts in on the next one. "Like they're all lined up, waiting for you."

I know what he means. Ever since seeing the old school, the names have been coming back to me, too. Joseph Yoon who lived in our neighborhood, Laura Wolfe who had gum stuck in her hair, Brodie Burris and Carter Kennedy. At lunch, a girl named Rachel would trade me her fruit punch drink.

And suddenly Dad's talking to me again.

"First thing we need to do is clean off the motor, oil the shaft, flip it over to the other side. Go ahead, take the C-clip off, that's the rusted thing there, we're going to pull the platter free. Be gentle now, this thing's been rusted for some time, no use treating it rough. All right, take out that spindle. Cycling gear's all seized up, but we'll get it working. All you really need is a needle, paper, and tape, and you'll hear some sound." And though I don't know what he's talking about, I'm listening to my dad, who seems happy for the first time in ages, and trying not to think about how it's time for dinner.

In the morning, Dad and I untie the rowboat from the porch and carry it down the hill, past the barn where our abandoned sailboat sits and our lawn slopes into the sea. He holds the rowboat as I climb in, hands me the oars, then climbs in himself, and we row across the waves, out past the tarpaper of neighbors' rooftops and into the open ocean. On the horizon, the old mall rises from the sea, and the cars in its flooded parking lot look like the shiny backs of horseshoe crabs.

A couple seagulls pass, squawking, and we stop at a buoy and pull up a rope. There's a batch of mussels clinging to the twine which I pick off in dark shiny handfuls, rattling them into the bucket between us. Dad lights a smoke and looks at the shopping plaza on the small island. There's the multiplex cinema and the old letters M CY'S and a handful of cars sitting above the tide line. There's plenty of goods still worth harvesting there, but the mall looks eerie with its shattered windows and jagged gateways to hidden caverns.

Before Mom left us, she took me to see a movie at that mall. Randy was with her. He bought me popcorn and took me into the theater, sat next to me until the coming attractions. "Hey," he said. "Your mom and I have to go do something—you'll be fine sitting here on your own, right? Just watch the movie, okay?" And Mom leaned across him. "We'll be back before the end. You don't need to pee, do you?" And I told her I didn't, even though I did. Then they left me in the darkness with the big tub of popcorn and a movie about animated mice that I can't even remember.

Dad smashes the window of a van with his hammer, then reaches in and pops the lock. He works on the radio until he's got the thing yanked out, an old model with wires which he inspects. "These ought to work," he says, and puts them in his bag before moving on to the next car, where he finds an old pack of cigarettes in the glove compartment. I grab the empty gas jugs from our rowboat and start in on the parked cars.

Snails cling to the windshields as I siphon the gas, their wet sucking sound a language none of us can understand. Most times the gas in these cars has already turned sour, but every once in a while we siphon out something good enough to filter that keeps our truck alive. Last winter our generator growled and coughed from old gas until it finally died, and I doubt the truck will make it much longer. All the same, I siphon. The first two come out brown, full of rust, but in the tank of a hatchback I smell the pine sharpness of good gas and start filling our jugs.

This mall reminds me of before the flood. How Dad pounded and sawed in the garage during those last months before Mom left. He bent the oak planks for our sailboat while my mother called him Noah, which he used to like, until she began saying it differently. After Mom disappeared, Dad took me sailing to search for her. He taught me how to raise the sails, catch the wind, and steer the tiller as he scanned the horizon. I didn't tell him that Mom had said Randy had a yacht in Newport. How she'd told me if the rains kept coming, it'd be real dry. How she'd promised to show it to me one day.

Dad and I searched for her for months, but there were no other boats on the ocean, just the roofs of evacuated houses and the tops of tall trees, which I navigated around. Eventually Dad gave up. We sailed back to the dock and loaded the boat onto his trailer, and he abandoned it in the barn. Dad said if we weren't going to escape with it, there was no good use for that ship. It was too large to navigate around the rooftops easily, and it reminded him too much of Mom. One night the tide lifted it off the ground and it bucked on the waves like a wild horse, kicking the barn with its bow and stern, rearing angrily against the walls. Dad waded in amid the thrashing, climbed aboard, and secured the sailboat with ropes to keep it from smashing itself to pieces. And I knew then that though the boat didn't bring him any joy, he didn't want to lose it, which is how I think he feels about me.

By the time the textbook is dry, the pages are wrinkled and hard to read, and I don't know why Dad wasted good diving time on it. I already know how to add, divide, subtract, and multiply; the book's useless unless he's thinking about using it for fire. All the same, he takes the book and the winter jacket and puts it in one of our good garbage bags. Then he wraps the turntable in another bag along with the records and takes them out to the truck, and I wonder if we're going to go see George who lives along the cape in a tiny waterlogged shack where he survives on seaweed, clams, and a woodshed full of bourbon he salvaged during the looting. But Dad doesn't drive in that direction. Instead he turns down South Road, which goes on for the longest stretch, curving around bends until it finally descends toward the sea. In summer, starfish cling to the windows of the houses down by the water's edge. We harvest them, and Dad fries them up, and we crack open their shells in the sunroom and chew out the spongy meat.

I've walked South Road alone on nights when the cloud cover's thin enough so you can almost see the moon, and I've explored the houses with their rotten stink from the fish that swim in during high tide and get stuck in the cabinets. In one of those houses was a boy's room. He had a Spiderman poster on the wall, and in a drawer I found a box with a Swiss Army knife, which I kept. But outside of that, there wasn't much to do except look out the windows at the empty island, everything looking haunted, and I realized how alone we were—just me and Dad and somewhere far down island, George drunk in his shack.

The rain is a fine mist, everything foggy and damp as Dad parks the truck. Down along the shoreline he shows me the small boathouse of an abandoned home, where a motorboat bobs on the tide. I can't believe he knew about this and never told me. We load the bags in. Dad fills the tank with new gas, pulls the cord until the motor coughs out smoke and catches, and he navigates us far from our truck, as though we'll never return to land.

"I'm going to introduce you to someone new today," he says after we've been chugging along for a while. "She lives across the sea. Her name's Dalia and she's got a little girl. They're also survivors. I want you to be polite to them."

Emerging from the mist like the bow of a ship is a

house on a small hill on another of the tiny islands that were once part of our township. It looks like there's a totem pole with massive wings in the front yard, but when we get closer I see it's a tall metal rod with blades attached, spinning slowly in the mist. Dad cuts the motor, guiding us toward a makeshift harbor. I splash out and help him pull our boat onto the shore and tie it to the base of the structure.

"What is this thing?" I ask.

"Wind turbine," Dad says. "Makes enough electricity to help them get through a day." He carries the bags along the flagstones toward the house where a woman stands in the doorway in a faded blue dress.

"Hey there, Josh," she says when we climb the steps. "I've been looking forward to meeting you." She extends her hand to me, and I wonder why she knows my name. Behind her is a little girl, holding on to her leg. "Her name's Fiona," the woman says.

"Hi," I say to the girl, but she just puts her face against her mom's dress.

Dad puts the bag down, unties it, and pulls out the puffy jacket. "Thought this might be a good fit for her." The girl looks at the jacket before reaching out to take it. "And a math book," Dad says, pulling out the crinkly textbook.

The woman takes it and looks through the pages. "Thank you."

"Here's the real prize, though." Dad reveals the turntable. "I fixed it. Should work all right with the electricity you have. It's a present for you." And the woman leans forward and gives him a kiss on his lips, so sudden it surprises me as much as if she'd hit him. I look down at the steps, understanding everything perfectly.

"You hungry, Josh?" the woman asks, carrying the turntable inside. "I'm making bluefish stew. We caught three of them this morning."

I step into her house, which is much nicer than ours. There's no dripping wetsuits over chair backs, no mildew stench or leaking windows, and the tabletops aren't covered with tools and empty conch shells. Seeing it makes me realize how messily Dad and I have been living. My room's full of fishing nets and drying socks. I don't think Mom would've let us live like that, and maybe that's the point, Dad trying to forget what it was like to live with her.

"Why don't you show Josh your room?" the woman says, and I follow Fiona, because doing that sounds way better than staying here with Dad and this woman who knows him well enough to kiss him.

Fiona's room has a plastic drawing table with a ceramic tea set on it, a couple of dolls, and a soccer ball. There's nothing I'm interested in, until she shows me a deck of playing cards on her shelf. "Want to play war? I'm missing the ace and a three."

"That's okay," I say. "I don't think it matters."

She moves the tea set off the plastic table and we sit in the small yellow chairs by the big window of her room overlooking the ocean. Along the small stretch of backyard are boxes with plastic bubbles over them. "What are those?" I ask.

"Mom grows potatoes and kale in them. You don't have a mom?" she asks, pushing her small pile of cards together with both hands.

"Yeah, I have a mom."

"Where is she?"

I look at the ocean. "Somewhere out there."

"My dad was out there, too, but I don't remember him; he drowned. Mom said you can't be sad forever or you'll drown from crying. You think your mom drowned?"

"No," I say, and lay down a jack to her queen.

Fiona takes her win. "We moved here because Mom said it would be good for catching the wind, but I liked our old house better. It's underwater now. Did you also steal someone's house?"

"No." I flip over the next card, a two of diamonds, which she takes with her five.

From the other room there's the sound of something scratching, then the sudden notes of music. Fiona and I get up to see what it is, and we find Dad and her mom standing by the wall where the turntable's plugged in. It spins the black disk around and around, letting out a squeal of horns.

"That's jazz," my father tells me, and I'm suddenly furious at him. There's been no music in our house for years, just the sound of rain, the pellet stove burning, and occasional thunder. The only instrument we have is Mom's old piano with its swelled dampers and stuck ivory keys, useless for anything but firewood and scrimshaw. It was like I'd forgotten there was such a thing as music, and now here it is, spilling into the living room as magical as if Dad had discovered sound itself, and I want to know why he's giving this miracle away to a stranger instead of me.

But I don't say any of that, I just stand there watching the machine spinning the record until the woman says the soup's ready, to come and get it.

In her kitchen, she takes a bowl and ladles out soup for me. The bowl's steaming hot against my hands, a stew with a fish head and big chunks of potato. I carry it to the wooden table in the living room, where the baseboard heaters let out a low rattle of warmth against my legs.

"Your dad says you're good at math," the woman tells me, which is news to me. I didn't know he'd told anyone anything, though the last couple of months suddenly make a lot more sense: the sound of Dad's truck starting up in the middle of the night, or him saying he was going to check the lobster traps and it'd be hours before he got back.

I shrug, though it's true. I've read the textbooks I had from ninth grade over and over, trying to figure out what would've come after algebra. I write notes in the margins and fill up the dead hours that stretch through our house by drawing angles and figuring out equations. "I like architecture."

"He told me." The woman gets up and goes to the bookshelf, takes a fat book down, and hands it to me.

"I thought maybe you'd like this." *Great Buildings of the World*. The hardcover isn't even waterlogged. I open the pages to a black-and-white photo of New York's Flatiron alongside a long description and the original blueprints.

"Wow," I say. There's a building called Fallingwater, one called the Dancing House, another named the Bird's Nest.

"Would you like it?"

I look at her. "Seriously? Yeah, thanks."

"Dalia was an engineer," my father says.

"Your dad said you might want to help me build another wind turbine. I can show you how. We'll have to raid some houses for parts, but that could be fun, right?"

"I guess," I say, still flipping through the pages, thinking how raiding with this woman doesn't sound like much fun at all.

"Thank you for the present," Dad says. "Now put away the book while we're eating." So I do, but for the rest of the meal all I can think about is how happy I am to have it.

It's getting dark by the time we leave. Outside, the world is murky in the wet dusk. Dad and the woman kiss, and then she and the little girl are standing on the steps, watching as we get into our boat, waving as we motor away through the darkness to our truck.

What's left of the island looks ominous as we drive home through the rain, just shadows of dead trees and the road slipping beneath us. The tide has returned, and there are sections where Dad has to drive across someone's lawn to get past the submerged street. Dad lights up a cigarette and its end glows orange in the cab, the cherry lighting his face so I can see how scrunched his brow is.

"Why didn't you tell me about them?"

Dad rolls down the window and ashes his cigarette. "I wanted to make sure she was important enough to introduce you to."

His answer makes no sense. Seems like meeting another two humans would be important enough to share no matter what. Also seems like if he had a warm place to go, it wasn't nice of him to leave me at home in our cold house which is damp and briny from seawater reducing on the stove.

"Why'd she get the turntable?"

"Because she has electricity, and I knew she'd like it," Dad says. "They're going to have dinner with us next week and sleep over."

"Why?"

"Because I invited them."

"Where are they going to sleep?"

"Dalia's going to sleep with me, and Fiona will be in your room."

"Why can't they sleep in the living room?"

"Because it's damp and we're not doing that. They're *guests*. You're going to share a room for a night. It's nice to share a room. You might need to get used to it."

And I don't say anything more to him the whole drive

home, not even when he wishes me good night. Instead, I light my candle and lie in bed, looking at the book the woman gave me. I flip the pages one by one, hearing the scratch of Dad's scrimshaw knife coming from below as he works on carving another piano key. There are pictures of Manhattan's skyscrapers, page after page of enormous buildings: the Empire State, the Chrysler, Rockefeller Plaza. I imagine those buildings rising above the ocean with whole neighborhoods surviving on upper floors fishing from windows, scanning the horizon, ready to welcome survivors like my mother, like me.

All week, Dad cleans out the house. He wipes off the tables, hauls oxygen tanks out to the garage, and makes me clear the fishing nets from my room. Our wetsuits disappear into closets, and I'm sent outside to work in the rain where I fill bucket after bucket with the oyster and conch shells we've let accumulate on our lawn until I'm soaked and hungry and angry that we're wasting time cleaning instead of fishing.

Dad boils water on the stove and fills big basins to rinse our clothes along with our sheets, wringing them out, though I know they'll never dry in time. Then we row out into the sea, pull up our lobster pots, and haul in four big green bugs, which sit in the kitchen sink, clawing at each other tiredly, their mouths bubbling foam as they try to escape up the stainless steel sides.

Our sheets are still damp on the night Dad picks up

Dalia and Fiona. I hear the truck return and watch the three of them getting out of the cab, my dad telling Fiona something that makes her laugh.

"We're here," Dad says as they come in. The woman says hello to me, and Dad takes their coats. "Why don't you show Fiona your room," he says.

"All right," I say, but what can I show her? Just baseball cards and a dumb graphic novel I'm bored with, though there's a globe that Fiona likes. I sit on the floor with her, spinning it slowly while she runs her fingers across the bumpy elevations, showing her what the earth looked like before the flood.

When we come down for dinner, the table's glowing with candlelight, so different from how our house usually looks that I hardly recognize it. Dad brings out the lobsters and we sit cracking their claws and using the small dish of salt that Dad made from boiled-down seawater. Mostly I'm thinking how weird everything feels. Dad sitting and talking about the old world with Dalia, something he never does with me. They're both being too gentle when they talk to me, like I'm a piece of bait they're trying to hook without getting barbed.

When dinner's over, I carry the pot of broken claws and picked-over bodies outside. The night is quiet, just the lull of the waves lapping against the barn with the incoming tide, and the sound of our sailboat rocking within. Inside, Dad's sitting with Dalia and Fiona around the candlelit table and it looks warm and cozy and completely foreign, like I'm gazing into some other family's house.

Even my own room looks unfamiliar with Fiona's makeshift mattress on the floor. When we go to bed, her mom comes in and kisses her on the forehead, which kind of hurts to watch, though she says good night to, too. Fiona's eyes are still open after her mom leaves. "You think there are mermaids in the ocean?" she asks, and I tell her no. Then she asks about the countries on the globe again, what their names are. After that, she asks what life was like before the flood.

"There were more people," I say. "Lots of kids, too. They'd ride bikes and you could go almost anywhere you wanted." I don't tell her about the toys floating in backseats or how neighbors fought for food in those last days before they drowned. Don't say how Dad dragged me past all those people in the flooded supermarket aisles, or how I saw a man punch another to reach a cereal box above the waterline. And I don't tell her how Mom disappeared with Randy on his yacht. But I do tell her about television, and how once upon a time there were stores upon stores with toys and electronics.

Fiona's asleep long before I get to the part about what the world down below looks like now. I lie in bed and listen to the rain tapping against the roof, and the sound of the waves outside. There's a low, stifled noise, which I finally place as the unfamiliar sound of my father's laughter. I can't hear what they're saying, so I get out of bed and sneak into the hallway, stepping carefully so as not to make the floor squeak.

"It's hard taking care of him alone," Dad says, speaking

softly like I haven't heard him talk to anyone except Mom. "She abandoned us, but he still misses her."

Taking care of me, I think. *I've been the one taking care of him all these years.*

"He's going to be okay," Dalia says. "And you don't have to do it alone anymore. We'll take care of each other. You think he'll want to come?"

"I'll talk to him. If I say we've got to move by spring, then that's how it'll be. The house is rotting anyway. He doesn't realize how little time we've got left."

And I understand, with the clarity of diving into cold water, how little I'm actually needed. Until a couple of days ago Dad hadn't even told me about this woman, and now he's planning to leave our house to be with her. Which is fine, because truth is, I've wanted to leave from the moment the floodwaters started rising. When everyone abandoned our neighborhood and Dad wouldn't evacuate, I climbed onto the roof and spelled out SOS with my clothes. I waved my arms, watching those helicopters disappear, while Dad stood out on the porch yelling for me to come down. "It's okay," he kept saying. "We don't need help."

I tiptoe back into my room where Fiona's sleeping, and I lie in my bed, looking out my window, trying to imprint what this house felt like to live in. The clouds look like schools of jellyfish through the window, drifting across the dark night, and behind them, somewhere, the moon. When I hear my father's snores, I crawl out of bed and open my closet. I get out my duffel bag and put my clothes in it, along with my rain jacket, my Swiss Army knife, and the architecture book.

The high tide is soft against the side of the barn, and when I pull the doors open through the water, the sail-boat is as still as a sleeping horse. I haul the tanks on, throw my duffel bag on deck, then climb aboard and untie the knots from the walls. The ship pulls toward the open sea, as though it also wants to leave, and once I raise the sail, it glides quietly through the water of our backyard. I know to navigate west, where eventually I'll hit land, and I know my father's happy now that he's with that woman. Maybe someday I'll sail home again, tell him everything I wrote in the note I left on my bed. How he doesn't need to worry about me. I've learned all the lessons he's tried to teach. I know how to dive and to hold my breath when the tanks run out, I know how to catch and gut fish, and I'll be okay without his help. Which is what I tell myself as the ship leaves our house behind. That it's okay for me to go; my life was never meant to be only with my father. I was always leaving anyhow, on my way toward some other world, full of strangers, one of them my mother, and a future, which like a deep-sea fish is out there wait-ing to be caught.

ACKNOWLEDGMENTS

I am deeply grateful for the love and support of so many people. Thank you to my agent extraordinaire, Leigh Feldman, and to Ilana Masad for futuristic guidance on these stories. Thank you to Caroline Zancan for making this collection sing and to the entire team at Henry Holt for ushering *Universal Love* into existence. Deep thanks to Phong Nguyen, Robert James Russell, and Stephen Weinstein for integral edits to early versions of these stories. To Howie Sanders, thank you for your intrepid championing. Deep thanks to Tony and Caroline Grant and the Sustainable Arts Foundation for everything you do to support parent-writers. Thank you to Siena Heights University for the gift of time which made this book possible. To Carol, Mark, Tina, and Laura for the LHSP/RC home. International love to Pablo Llambías, Rúnar Helgi Vignisson, Mads Bunch, and Lárus Jón Guðmundsson. Endless gratitude to the writers at the Martha's Vineyard Institute of Creative Writing for building a community with magic and love every summer. To my friends, who've surrounded me with the warmth of your hearts during the writing of this book—Nicholas, Brodie and Carter, Frank and Larissa, Hosef (edible insect love), Milagros and Curtis (proofing love), Craig Holt (coffee love), David and Priscilla, Jill, Jayne, Clay, the A2, Geneseo, and MV crew, and so many others. Wopila to Harold Thompson, Iam and Laura, Stef and Kathy, and the Ypsilanti lodge community. For Mason, Ashton, Blake, and the Higginses and Brotjes—your love means the world to me. Universal love across the sea to my Danish and English family. To my parents for a lifetime of love and guidance. To Rachel, love of my life, for this lifetime and infinite more. To my son, Peter, light of my life and first listener to these stories. And to all of you, thank you for making this world a better place with your love.